The
Only
Way
Out

Other titles by Deborah Kent
you will enjoy:

Too Soon to Say Good-bye

Why Me?

One Step at a Time

The Only Way Out

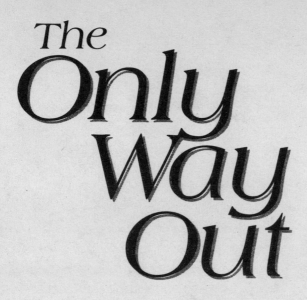

Deborah Kent

AN
APPLE
PAPERBACK

SCHOLASTIC INC.
New York Toronto London Auckland Sydney

ISBN 0-590-54081-5

12 11 10 9 8 7 6 5 4 3 2 1   7 8 9/9 0 1 2/0

Printed in the U.S.A.   40
First Scholastic printing, August 1997

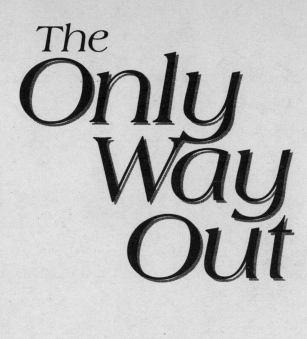

The Only Way Out

1

"No fair!" Virginia screeched. "You can't tag me! I'm home free!"

"You are not!" I insisted, gripping her by the strap of her pink corduroy overalls. "Home is the slide, remember?"

"Not anymore. Now home free is the ground! You've got to tag me when I'm in the air!"

I let go and flopped onto the grass. "I give up! This is too much!"

She's only five years old, I reminded myself. And I'm fourteen, her baby-sitter, the person in charge. I couldn't let her get the better of me.

Unfortunately, it wasn't that easy. Virginia was in control, and she knew it. At lunch, she'd rejected the hot dog I cooked for her, and insisted on a peanut butter and baloney sandwich instead. Then she'd refused to draw with the colored pencils I brought, and demanded a trip to the park. Her mother had said we could go if Virginia was a good girl. In my opinion, she didn't qualify. But here we were, playing tag in the broiling midday sun. And Virginia kept changing the rules.

"Maybe you can get me when I'm running," she went on. "When I run, I leap up in the air a lot."

Virginia dashed to the jungle gym, leaping as she went. Like a monkey she scrambled to the top. "You'll never get me up here!" she called. "I'm higher than you can reach!"

I sat up and pushed my hair back from my face. A mother with a little boy watched disapprovingly from over by the sandbox. "Come on, Shannon!" Virginia yelled. "Catch me!"

Taunting me, she swayed to and fro on her high steel bar. I had to do something. I was responsible for her safety. If her hold slipped, there was nothing but empty space between her and the ground, six feet below.

I sprang to my feet. "Come down," I said. "We're leaving."

"What?"

"We're going *now*," I said. I stepped toward her and waited, hands on my hips. I tried to look menacing.

"No!" Virginia cried. "You can't make me!"

"I mean it!" I told her. "One . . . two . . . three!"

She stared at me, daring me to do something. I gazed back helplessly. Why should she listen to me? She knew I was powerless.

The woman by the sandbox was still looking on. Now she gestured for the little boy to stay where he was. He waited obediently with his pail and shovel as she strode toward us. "You need a hand?" she asked me.

"Well, maybe," I answered.

The woman fixed her gaze upon Virginia. "Get down from there this instant, young lady," she commanded. "No more fooling around."

Virginia swung free, dangling by her hands. Then, with a soft thud, she dropped to the ground. "Do I have to go home?" she said, pouting. She looked to the woman for an answer, not to me.

"Yes," I said, trying to make my voice strong and stern. I felt my cheeks flush, and it wasn't from the heat. It was humiliating to thank this stranger for rescuing me, but I did it all the same. Then I grabbed Virginia's hand. I marched her out of the park before she could think of some new way to torment me.

What was the matter with me? I asked myself later, as I walked home from Virginia's house. I couldn't stand up to a spoiled five-year-old. Even a little kid like Virginia knew that I was a mouse. I was afraid of strangers. I was afraid of teachers, nurses, doctors. Worst of all, I was afraid of most kids my own age. The world always seemed to be turning too fast, trying to spin me off my feet. I was never sure I could keep my balance.

This year would be different, I promised myself. I'd be starting high school, plunging into a new environment where nobody knew who I was.

No one would feel sorry for me. No one would think of me as poor Shannon Thomas, the kid with Hodgkin's disease, hanging at the brink of death. No one would collect money to send flowers to my hospital room. No delegation of class officers would come to pay me a tense fifteen-minute visit. This year I would start fresh, and I would become the person I wanted to be.

I opened the back door and stepped into the kitchen. "Mom?" I called. No answer. The house had a bleak, empty feeling, and I knew that no one was home. I popped a frozen chicken dinner into the microwave and sat down to my solitary supper. I didn't mind being by myself. It gave me plenty of time to think.

If I could be anybody, I'd be Julie Raskin. I'd known Julie since fifth grade, but we weren't friends. She headed the popular crowd, and all I could do was watch her from a distance. Whatever she said made people laugh. Wherever she went, people pushed to sit next to her, to walk beside her, to catch a little of her glow. I still didn't understand her secret. But this year I'd have a chance to find the answer. This year I was well at last.

I was a little small for my age going into sixth grade, but I was never sick. I could never persuade Mom that I had a stomachache on the morning of a math test; my temperature was dis-

4

couragingly normal when she tested me with the thermometer. The only time I ever saw the doctor was when I needed a physical for school. That was why I went to Dr. McHale that fall, to have him fill out some routine form for the school nurse to file in my permanent record.

I remember sitting on the doctor's padded table, glancing around at the posters on the walls. One showed a Pekinese dog like a walking haystack, with the caption, "And I thought *I* was having a bad hair day!" I patted my own hair into place as best I could. It was light brown, curly and thick, and it had a will of its own.

Finally Dr. McHale came in. He was kind of old and grayish, about forty-five, my father's age. While he peered into my eyes, ears, and throat, he asked me a string of questions. What grade was I in this year? Who was my teacher? What was my favorite subject? Any boyfriends yet? My answers were as predictable as the questions were. "Sixth grade. . . . Mrs. Kozlowski. . . . Reading. . . . No, the boys in my class are all gross."

"You won't say that two years from now," Dr. McHale said knowingly. He slid his hand along my jawbone and down the side of my neck.

"You haven't met these boys," I began. "They're all weirdos." Suddenly I realized that Dr. McHale wasn't listening. I felt his fingers pause somewhere below my left ear. They probed, concentrated, sought something out.

5

"Turn your head this way," the doctor said brusquely. "Okay, now the other way." He felt around in the same spot under my right ear, then went back to the left side again.

"What's wrong?" I asked.

"Probably nothing," Dr. McHale said. "Have you had a sore throat or anything lately? Any kind of a virus?"

I shook my head. "No, I've been fine."

"Your mother's in the waiting room, isn't she?"

I nodded. Dr. McHale stepped to the door, and in a moment Mom joined us. He got straight to the point. "She has a very enlarged lymph node in her neck," he said. "Most likely it's nothing to get alarmed about. But I want to see her back in ten days or so, just to get another look."

"What *is* a lymph node?" I demanded. I'd never known I had such a thing, enlarged or otherwise.

"It's sort of like a gland," the doctor explained. "Lymph nodes are scattered all over the body. They manufacture phagocytes — those are cells that destroy germs and keep you from getting sick."

"What does it mean if a lymph node is enlarged?" Mom asked.

"Nothing, most likely," said Dr. McHale. "Probably there's a virus in her system somewhere, and she's fighting it off. We want to keep tabs on it, that's all."

"Why?" I asked. "Could it be something bad?" I

was curious. I'd never had anything worse than chickenpox in my life. Somehow all this concern was interesting.

"I doubt it very much," Dr. McHale said reassuringly. "The chances that it's anything to worry about are maybe one in a thousand."

I felt perfectly well. It was hard to understand why everyone was making such a fuss. My enlarged lymph node was nothing but a small, painless lump. It felt like a lima bean nestled beneath my skin. But the doctors took it very seriously. They stopped saying "enlarged lymph node" and began to use the ominous word *tumor.*

After several appointments and an overnight stay in the hospital, I received the final diagnosis: Hodgkin's disease.

I had never heard of Hodgkin's disease before. But from the way the specialists uttered the name, I knew it was something I didn't want. It would require "very extensive treatment," they explained. They said a lot of things I couldn't take in, but the words had a sinister ring. *Surgery. Radiation. Chemotherapy.* And always one massive word looming over everything else: CANCER.

Over the past three years, I'd learned more than I ever wanted to know about my illness and its treatment. Hodgkin's disease was a form of cancer that attacked the lymph system. Without treatment, I would only live a year. But treatment

7

for my condition was improving all the time, the doctors assured me. Today my chances were very encouraging. Very encouraging indeed.

I had three surgeries to remove enlarged lymph nodes from my neck and under my arms. I had radiation treatments — heavy doses of X rays — to destroy any cancer cells that might still be lurking around after the operations. And I had round after round of chemotherapy. "Chemo," as they called it in the hospital, was extremely powerful medication. It was supposed to kill cancer cells, "the bad guys," as Dr. O'Brien liked to call them. The trouble was, it almost killed me at the same time.

Dr. O'Brien was my pediatric oncologist, which is a fancy way to say she was a doctor for kids with cancer. She talked a lot about "bad guys" and "good guys." The bad guys were the cancer cells that had invaded my body. Nobody could tell me how they got in. But they were with me now, and they wanted to take control. If we didn't stop them, they'd wipe out my liver, my spleen, my kidneys, and sooner or later I would die. The good guys were the healthy cells, the ones fighting to keep me alive. Sometimes when Dr. O'Brien explained it, I sensed the battle raging inside me. I pictured the bad guys as slimy little creatures with crawling tentacles. The good guys were gallant warriors on horseback. They shot the bad guys with arrows and made them disappear. Dr.

O'Brien smiled when I described those scenes to her. She called it "imaging," and said it could help my immune system fight harder.

"If my immune system can win this fight, why do I have to have chemo?" I asked her. It was one of those times when they had me in the hospital. Medications dripped from a tier of bottles at the foot of my bed and flowed toward me through coils of clear plastic tubing. Drop by drop they slid through a needle into a vein in my arm. The drugs seemed to burn their way all through me. I felt them poisoning me from my scalp to the soles of my feet. My vision blurred. Every joint and muscle ached, and I was so nauseous I hardly dared to speak.

"I wish it worked that way," Dr. O'Brien sighed. "I wish chemo wasn't necessary. But your immune system needs all the help it can get right now."

This isn't help, I wanted to scream. This is torture! How could dying be any worse?

Those years of illness and treatment changed my view of the world. I saw myself as a powerless victim, unable to make choices. And people treated me like a stranger. The kids at school were polite and cautious, as if I wasn't really one of them any longer. Hodgkin's disease ruled my life. I could only submit to whatever treatment plan the doctors devised.

The drugs *did* help in the end. I had no more lumps. My bone marrow tests and blood count were in the normal range once more. At my last appointment three weeks before, Dr. O'Brien announced that I was in remission.

One thing about cancer doctors — they never say you're cured. Remission is about the best news they're willing to offer. But by now I knew what that meant. It meant there was no longer any trace of cancer in my body.

"How long is this remission going to last?" I wanted to know.

"There's no way to predict," Dr. O'Brien said, with her usual caution. "It'll be five years before we're sure you're free and clear. If you notice any more tumors — or if you have any other symptoms — it's very important that you contact us right away. Don't lose valuable time."

She paused to let her warning sink in. Then, her duty out of the way, Dr. O'Brien smiled. "This remission could last for years," she said. "It might even be permanent."

I wanted to forget all of the warnings. I wanted to rush out of Dr. O'Brien's office and begin the rest of my life as though cancer had never touched me. But I knew what she was trying to say. She offered hope, but she couldn't make promises.

The front door banged as I was rinsing my dishes. Mom came in with an armload of groceries she'd picked up on her way home from work.

"How was Virginia?" she asked, thumping the bags down on the counter.

"The usual," I said. I put the new jug of milk into the fridge. "How was work?"

"Okay," Mom said. "Oh, I have to tell you — I've got some good news and some bad news."

"What is it?" I asked, giving her my full attention. "Let me have the good news first."

"The good news," Mom said, breaking into a smile, "is you won second place in the Arts Foundation contest!"

"I *what?*"

"You heard me," Mom said, laughing. "I got a call this morning before I left the house. They're going to put your pictures in an exhibition at the Capitol Building. Oh, and some reporter's supposed to call tonight. They want to run a story in the paper."

I'd missed a lot of school over the past three years. When I was too sick to go out, but well enough to feel bored, I drew pictures. I had always loved to draw. I even took classes at an art school for a while. After I got sick, Dad brought home a lot of books on art, and I learned everything I could. Sometimes I drew scenes from novels. Sometimes I sketched Mom or Dad, or our cats Pixie and Madge. One of my teachers talked me into entering a contest run by the Wisconsin Arts Foundation. "You can't win if you don't en-

11

ter," she pointed out. Obediently I chose half a dozen pictures, packed them up, and sent them off. I never thought I had a chance. But I was afraid of what my teacher would say if I refused to give it a try.

"What did I win, anyway?" I asked Mom.

"You don't know?" Mom asked. "Second prize is five hundred dollars!"

I grabbed the phone and called Abby, my best friend. Abby was one of those people who got really excited about little things. For something as big as this, she nearly turned herself inside out, shouting and cheering and asking questions. By the time I hung up, I could hardly think straight myself. But a dim, troubling thought managed to break through.

"There was something else you had to tell me," I said. "What was the *bad* news?"

"Oh," Mom said brightly, as if it hardly mattered. "Dr. O'Brien's taking a new job in California. When you go for your checkup next time, you'll see Dr. Calder, Dr. O'Brien's replacement."

2

I was sorry to learn that Dr. O'Brien was leaving. As much as I could like a doctor, I liked her. She was warm and smiling beneath her nononsense veneer. Of course I hadn't expected to see her very often anymore, now that I was in remission. But I still had to go for a checkup every few weeks. I could hardly imagine starting over with a stranger.

I had no idea just how much I would miss Dr. O'Brien until I went to see Dr. Calder.

Dr. Calder's office was in the outpatient department at the hospital, the same building where I used to see Dr. O'Brien. Everything felt familiar as Mom and I took the elevator up to the fifth floor. But instead of turning right and walking into Dr. O'Brien's waiting room, we had to search for Room 526. We made three wrong turns before I finally spotted it, next to the fire door at the end of a long, white corridor.

"You have an appointment scheduled for Shannon Thomas?" Mom asked the receptionist.

Dr. O'Brien's receptionist, Judy, always broke out in smiles when we came in. Once I gave her a papier-mâché clown that I had made in Girl Scouts, and she kept it on her desk. Even when I knew I might hear bad news from Dr. O'Brien, news about my next round of chemotherapy, Judy made me feel good.

I didn't know Dr. Calder's receptionist, and she didn't know me. "Thomas," she muttered, glancing through a list of names. "Yes, she's down for three forty-five. Take a seat."

Dr. O'Brien always had good music on in her waiting room. The Top Ten made the atmosphere a little less medical. Dr. Calder's waiting room was washed in the syrupy violins of some "easy-listening" station. I guess that kind of music is supposed to relax you. It just put me on edge. It made me feel as if something bad was waiting to catch me off guard.

We had the whole waiting room to ourselves. "He must not have many patients," I said to Mom as we sat down. "Maybe he's not that good."

Mom frowned and put her finger to her lips, as if she thought the place might be bugged. My mother was very careful to stay on the good side of doctors. Dad, on the other hand, walked in with a list of questions. If he didn't think the answers

14

made sense, he'd throw himself into a fight. But Mom was quiet, polite, submissive. "You don't want them to think you're a troublemaker," she told me once. "They might not try quite as hard to help you."

"They've *got* to help you, it's their job," I protested.

Mom shook her head. "Sure it is," she said. "But I want them to do *more* than their job. They're taking care of *my* daughter!"

I took a seat, picked up a magazine, and tried to block out the rendition of "Moon River" that oozed from the overhead speakers. The longer I sat there, the more nervous I became. This is just a routine checkup, I reminded myself. You've had dozens of them before. But I was getting a bad feeling in my stomach. Nothing good would come of this.

The door from the corridor opened. I glanced up to see a tall, thin girl walk in with a boy who must have been her older brother. She wore shorts and a purple tank top, and looked to be about fifteen. I knew right away that she was the patient. Her face looked puffy and blotched, the way mine did whenever they put me on a drug called prednisone. And her head was covered with dark fuzz. Her hair was just beginning to grow back. I knew what that was like. Twice I'd lost all of my hair as a grisly side effect of chemo. Twice I'd gone

15

through that prickly, itchy stage of waiting for it to come back in.

"Sit over here, Kim," the boy said. "Mom said to start your homework, don't forget."

Homework in July? I wondered. Then I knew. She was taking a summer make-up course because she'd missed so much school this past year.

The girl called Kim made a face at her brother. "I'll get it done," she said, and dropped her schoolbag into the corner. For a moment she sat quietly, her hands on her lap. Then she looked over at me. "Hey," she said. "I never saw you here before. You go to Dr. Calder too?"

"No," I said. "I mean yeah. Starting today."

I was no good at talking to people I didn't know. Uselessly I rifled through my mind for something else to say. Kim watched me for a moment, shrugged, and leafed through a magazine.

"Have you got math?" her brother asked. "Mom said if you've got math you better get started this afternoon."

"It's summer school," Kim said. "The old rules don't apply."

Maybe she just wanted to get away from her brother's nagging. Anyway, she turned to me again. "I've been seeing this doctor for six months, and I'm still not better," she declared. She almost sounded proud of herself.

"It takes way longer than six months," I told her. "Three to five years. That's what they always told me."

"That's stupid," Kim said. "It doesn't have to take that long. If you know where to go, you can get better just like that!" She snapped her fingers.

"What do you mean?" I asked, bewildered.

"Shannon Thomas?" the receptionist called, poking her head through the door. "Down the hall in Room Eight."

"I'll go in with her, since it's her first time," Mom said.

The receptionist nodded. I waved good-bye to Kim, and Mom and I headed down the hall. We sat in a strange, bare office with a diploma from the University of Kansas Medical School on the wall. A nameless nurse took my temperature and checked my blood pressure. "The doctor will be right with you," she said, and we waited some more.

The moment Dr. Calder walked in, I wondered why I had felt so apprehensive. He was the youngest-looking doctor I'd ever seen, with dark wavy hair, long eyelashes, and a truly sparkling smile. He looked more like a rock star than an M.D. He was the kind of guy whose picture Abby pinned on her bulletin board. And he was nice. To my amazement, he was easy to talk to.

"So you're the famous artist!" he exclaimed. "I read about you in the paper!"

"They got my age wrong," I said, blushing. "They said I'm fifteen, and I'm fourteen really."

"But you won a statewide contest," Dr. Calder said. "They got that much right. That's pretty exciting!"

"Yeah," I said. "I still can't believe it." I hesitated. "I wish they didn't put in about my having cancer, though. They made such a big deal out of it."

"You know the media," Dr. Calder sighed. "I guess it's what they call human interest."

"It's not interesting to me," I told him. "I'd just as soon forget about it."

"Dr. O'Brien told me about you, too," he said, picking up my chart. "She said you were really brave going through your treatment."

"I wasn't brave," I said. "I was miserable. I hated every minute of it."

"Well, who can blame you for that?" he asked. "It's no day at the beach."

He sat down and read through my record for a long, silent minute. It was very thick, and he flipped fast through the pages. At last he set the folder down and turned back to me and Mom.

"Things are looking pretty good," he said, addressing both of us this time. "But that last bone marrow — the numbers are just borderline."

18

"Dr. O'Brien said I was fine!" I burst out. "I'm in remission!"

Mom held up her hand to silence me. This was our very first visit, and already I was arguing with the doctor. It made her extremely nervous.

"It's a matter of interpreting the numbers," Dr. Calder explained. "A lot of my colleagues would agree with Dr. O'Brien. But there are some new findings. People with numbers in your range seem to do better with some changes in the treatment protocol."

I didn't have a clue what he was talking about. I just sat there looking at him. I remember thinking how I'd describe his eyelashes to Abby. She had a real thing for guys with long lashes.

"What sort of changes, exactly?" Mom asked.

"You understand what I mean by the protocol?" Dr. Calder said. "With any medical condition, there are certain standard treatment procedures, agreed upon by all the major hospitals. With Hodgkin's disease, it's accepted that we give x amount of one medication over x number of months, and y amount of another one over y number of months. You follow me so far?"

"I think so," Mom said. "Dr. O'Brien explained things to us as we went along."

"Well, those protocols are based on statistics," Dr. Calder continued. "They tally up all the fig-

19

ures from around the country, and try to calculate what works best for the greatest number of patients."

"Yeah," I said. "Dr. O'Brien drew us a little graph one time." I wanted him to know I was paying attention.

"Good," he said, beaming his smile in my direction. "You've got it so far. Now, all over the world there's research going on. We're learning more about cancer every day. We're constantly improving the methods for treating it, so that more people will survive longer."

Even then, I didn't suspect what was coming. I thought this was just Dr. Calder's way of getting acquainted.

But Mom must have sensed something. She sat up a little straighter in her chair. "Is there something new we ought to know about?" she asked eagerly. "Have they got something better now for Hodgkin's?"

"There was a report published a couple of weeks ago," Dr. Calder said. "Some very encouraging results out of Houston. For patients with these borderline numbers, they're recommending an extension to the standard chemotherapy regimen."

"This report says she should have . . . some more chemotherapy?" Mom asked. She studied my face, watching for my reaction. I felt as if someone had just knocked me on the head with a brick. I was too stunned to open my mouth.

Dr. Calder watched me, too. "I know you'd rather have the whole business over with," he said kindly. "But we've got to look at what's best in the long run."

"But I'm all right!" I found my voice at last. "Dr. O'Brien said I didn't need any more chemo!"

"In this study, seventeen percent of the Hodgkin's patients who got the extended treatment outlived the patients who didn't."

"Seventeen percent," Mom repeated. "That's seventeen out of every one hundred."

"It's significant!" Dr. Calder sounded excited, as if he were offering us a present. "They survived up to three years longer, on average."

"Wait a second!" I exclaimed. "Dr. O'Brien said I could be okay for years as it is. She said maybe this remission could be permanent."

"We certainly hope that's true," Dr. Calder said. "It very well may be." He paused for emphasis. "But cancer's a rough game. You never know for sure who's winning. I'd like to see you have the best possible chance to live a long time and do all the things you want to do."

"What sort of treatment are we talking about?" Mom asked. "When would it start?"

"I know you'll want time to talk this over at home," Dr. Calder said. "But if we decide to go ahead I'd like to get started within the next two weeks."

"I have to go back on chemo again?" I cried. "In two weeks I've got to go back?"

"Wouldn't you rather get the first round over before school starts?" Dr. Calder asked. "That way you won't get behind." He looked like an M.D. now — important, powerful, full of intentions. He was in control. He could change the rules as he chose.

Starting high school was going to be my fresh opportunity. I thought I could become someone new. Now I'd just be the same old Shannon Thomas — out sick every other day, my face puffed up and blotchy. I'd probably go bald again. I didn't stand a chance.

I wasn't good at speaking up for myself. But suddenly I was almost shouting. "I don't want to do it before school starts! I don't want to do it *after* school starts either! I don't want any more chemotherapy, period!"

"Shannon!" Mom said, shocked. "You have to be mature about this."

"What's the use?" I demanded. "Mature means I do whatever you tell me, right? Be a good girl and take my medicine! I *did* that, and what good did it do me? I spent half my time throwing up and wishing I could die and get it over with!"

For three years I had been good and patient, and maybe even a little brave sometimes. I had earned my reward, my remission. Now they said my remission wasn't good enough.

"We'll talk this over with Dad," Mom said. "We'll try to make the best decision we can."

"I don't care about some stupid percent," I told them. "I'm through with chemotherapy!"

3

"On the basis of one study? Dad asked. "Isn't this guy jumping on the bandwagon?"

"Yeah," I said. "Dr. O'Brien said I was in remission."

They didn't seem to hear me. "Well, he said these new findings are significant," Mom said.

Their words floated above me as I sprawled on the carpet with my sketch-pad. Back and forth they went, questioning, challenging, settling my fate. My vote didn't count. They would decide what was best for me — Mom and Dad and Dr. Calder.

Mom was for the extra chemo. She said they couldn't ignore anything that might improve my chances. As usual, Dad was the one who held back at first. He wanted more information. Doctors were notorious for pushing every new treatment, he insisted. A year from now, they might come out with a study claiming the less chemo the better. At that my heart gave a happy little skip. But then Mom said, "You read the article Dr. Calder sent us. These people in Houston are the best in the country." I put down my pencil and lay with my eyes closed, drained of hope.

"We'll work it out Monday," Dad said at last. "What time is our conference again?"

"Eleven," Mom said. She always wrote appointments down on the calendar, but she never had to look at it. She carried them around in her head.

"Monday at eleven," Dad said. "We'll both talk to this Dr. Calder and whatever colleagues he brings in. We'll think it through."

"I've thought it through, if anybody's interested," I said from the floor. "I've had enough treatment already."

Mom reached down and ruffled my hair. "If I made the rules, nobody would *ever* have to have chemo," she said. "But if I were in charge, nobody would ever get Hodgkin's disease, either."

"We're going to figure this out," Dad said. "We'll learn everything we can, and make an educated decision."

"*We* won't," I muttered. "*You* will." But nobody seemed to hear me.

Monday morning came much too soon. Dad and Mom both took time off from work, and we drove to the hospital in silence. This time we only made one wrong turn to find Room 526. The receptionist recognized me today, but she didn't remember my name. "Sharon, you can take a seat in the waiting room," she told me. To Dad and Mom she said, "The conference room is down the hall and to your right. They're ready for you."

The same easy-listening music washed over the waiting room, but there were more people than last time. A man in a business suit pored over papers on a clipboard, while a woman who must have been his wife sat filing her nails. To take my mind off my worries, I tried playing detective. Which one of them was the cancer patient? They both looked pale for July, but both of them had plenty of hair — unless he was wearing a wig . . .

I leaned forward, trying to get a better view. The man's hair seemed a bit too neat, too perfectly symmetrical. Maybe it wasn't really his own. On the other hand, his wife's face was thin and bony, as though she were losing weight . . .

The door burst open. I glanced up, eager for another distraction. In walked Kim, stubbly hair and all. Her brother was with her again, and this time their mother had come, too.

"See?" Kim said, glancing around. "There are all these people ahead of me. What did we rush for?"

"What did I have to *come* for?" her brother wanted to know. "I could have been playing baseball."

"Settle down, both of you," the mother said with a sigh. "Fight, fight, fight! Fight with the

26

traffic, fight with the two of you — it's exhausting!"

"Well, at least I get out of classes today," Kim said cheerfully. She flopped onto a leather sofa and kicked her feet in the air.

"Sit up nicely!" he mother said. "Don't drape yourself all over the furniture."

The woman with the nail file glanced up, frowning. Somehow Kim and her family changed the whole atmosphere of the waiting room. The syrupy music was drowned beneath their noise and confusion.

Kim straightened up and placed her feet side by side on the floor. "Can we tell him today?" she asked. "I want to see the look on his face!"

Her mother sighed again. "I'd just as soon keep it to ourselves," she said. "I don't need a fight with the doctor, on top of everything else."

"I can't believe you guys are serious about this!" the brother exclaimed. "I thought it was just some crazy idea Grandma got out of a magazine."

"Coming here is what's crazy!" Kim said, kicking the leg of her chair. "Getting dosed with rat poison week after week!"

I felt almost invisible, sitting there observing them. It was like watching a play. But suddenly Kim called me out of the audience. "Hey," she said, "I saw you the last time I was here. What'd you think of old Dr. C?"

"He's okay," I said.

If I didn't say something else, Kim would give up on me. And I really wanted to talk to her. What would Julie Raskin say in this situation?

"He's okay to look at, anyway," Kim remarked, giving me one last chance.

"Yeah," I said, "he'd be gorgeous if he'd pick some other job." I didn't even tell Abby about his long eyelashes after all.

Kim grinned. She got up and took a seat next to mine. "The practice of medicine ruins the nicest people," she said. "What a waste."

Mom and Dad were talking to Dr. Calder this very minute. He'd even brought in some of his doctor buddies. They were all in the conference room, making an educated decision. A decision about me.

Kim said all this chemotherapy was stupid. She said you could be cured in the snap of a finger, if you knew where to go.

How much longer would the conference last, I wondered. I had to ask Kim a question. Would I have enough time?

"When I saw you here before," I began cautiously, "we were talking about how long it takes to get better . . ."

"Yeah," Kim said. "They told me that three to five years stuff, too."

"And you said . . . something about . . ." I had

the feeling I was poised on a high ledge, ready to leap into the unknown. "You said you knew another way, that was quicker."

"Sister Euphrasia," Kim said. She lowered her voice. "She has the gift."

"What gift?" I asked. I lowered my voice, too.

"The gift of healing," Kim said. "Some people have it. Nobody knows why. They put their hands on you in a certain way, and the disease goes right out of your body."

I sighed. I felt as weary as Kim's mother. Laying on of hands . . . a diet of tofu and rice . . . gazing into crystals to put my aura in balance. . . . Over the past three years, I'd heard it all. My cousin Rena relayed every new promise from every call-in show on the radio dial. I'd stuck with the tofu and rice for a whole week, full of high hopes. Every meal was a battle with Mom and Dad. Dad said, Wasn't Hodgkin's disease bad enough? Did I want beriberi, too? When they took me back to Dr. O'Brien, I had lost four pounds. She said if I kept it up they'd have to put me in the hospital to bring up my weight. There weren't any miracle cures, she said sadly, and I believed her.

"Lots of people say they can heal you," I told Kim. "My dad says they ought to be thrown in jail for preying on desperate people."

"There are fakes around," Kim agreed. "But Sister Euphrasia's for real."

"Why? What's real about her?" I was starting to sound like Dad, tossing out questions, raising a challenge. I'd forgotten all about being shy.

"My grandmother knows this lady that went to her," Kim said. "She'd had six operations for cancer, and the doctors gave up on her. Then she went to Sister Euphrasia and got better. If you don't believe me, ask my grandmother!"

"Maybe it was really the operations," I said. "Sister Euphrasia probably had nothing to do with it."

"I'm glad to hear somebody talking sense!" Kim's brother said from across the room. I'd become so caught up in our discussion that I'd forgotten we weren't alone. My cheeks flushed red-hot.

"Who asked you, Jonathan?" Kim snapped.

"Somebody has to be the voice of reason around here," Jonathan said.

Kim turned back to me. "It's not just that one lady," she said. "There are hundreds of cases. A bunch of scientists went down to study her, and they couldn't explain it."

"Did they think she could really heal people?" I asked. It couldn't be true, but I still wished Kim would convince me.

"That's what I'm trying to tell you!" Kim said. "They examined the people who went to Sister Euphrasia, and looked at their hospital records and everything, and they couldn't understand it.

All these people who were supposed to have cancer were perfectly normal."

"No more chemo?" I marveled. "No more radiation?"

Kim waved her hand in farewell. "Nope," she said. "Bye-bye."

My heart jumped with excitement. "You're going to see her? You're going to try it?"

"As soon as my mom gets the money together," Kim said. "For the airfare, and someplace to stay and all that. I can't wait to tell Dr. C."

I thought of Mom, the way she tried to stay on the doctor's good side. "He won't like it," I warned her. "He might get mad at you."

Kim threw back her shoulders. "So what?" she asked. "I won't need him anymore."

"Just don't forget that Grandma believes in flying saucers, too," Jonathan put in.

"Why are you like this?" Kim demanded. "You don't want me to go, do you?"

Jonathan was silent. He looked down at his hands. "I just hate for you to get all psyched up about this," he said at last. "I don't want to see you be disappointed."

"Shannon Thomas," the receptionist called. "You can go down to the conference room now. They want to talk to you."

I must have stood up too fast. The room spun. I nearly tripped over the man with the clipboard.

"Down the hall and to your right," the receptionist said at my back. Dad stood outside the conference room, beckoning. I followed him inside, and he waved me toward a chair. I sat down at a long table. It was dotted with papers and Styrofoam coffee cups, but still it seemed bare and cold. There were three doctors I'd never seen, plus Dr. Calder. I didn't look at any of them. Mom sat across from me. She gave me a tight smile, but I didn't smile back.

"Hi, Shannon," Dr. Calder began brightly. "I guess you're a little nervous, wondering what this big powwow is about. So we thought you should come in, and we could explain a few things and let you ask questions."

I didn't answer. Finally Mom said, "Dr. Calder, maybe you can start by telling her what we've decided to do."

Dr. Calder cleared his throat. "You remember I told you and your mom about the new study that shows — " He paused. "Shannon, are you listening?"

"Yeah," I said, turning to face him at last.

"Okay," he said. "Now, you're not really anemic. Your blood count is in the normal range, but it's low normal. The study shows that people with counts like yours do better if they get additional chemotherapy."

I nodded. He went on. "Well, we want you to have all the advantages, the best treatment possible. So after talking it over, we decided to put you on the new treatment program."

Everyone stared at me, waiting for me to speak. But my words wouldn't make any difference.

"Shannon?" Dad asked. "Do you have any questions?"

I shook my head.

"Are you sure?" said Mom.

"Positive," I said.

There was a long silence.

"Well then," Dr. Calder said, "we'll set up a schedule. You'll have to go back into the hospital for a week or so. The first medications have to be given intravenously."

IV chemo. I knew what that meant. I'd be helpless, flat on my back, with a needle dripping rat poison into my arm. That's what Kim called it — rat poison. It would burn through my veins and gnaw my guts till it made me writhe and gag and vomit and wonder what was the use of staying alive.

Dr. Calder went on about pills I would take at home, and how in a couple of months it would all be over. Finally the doctors gathered their files, murmuring about the next meeting they had to attend. For them this was all routine, just part of the day's work.

Dad put his arm across my shoulders, as if to

steady me on my feet. Mom stepped in beside us, and together we headed for the door. Dr. Calder stopped us in the hall. "I know how awful it is — all this chemotherapy," he told me. "I'm sorry you have to go through it again. I really am."

My eyes blurred with tears. If only I could hate him! But Dr. Calder was on my side. They all were.

Out in the waiting room, Mom and Dad went to the receptionist to set up my next appointment. I'd have to come in for more blood work before I went to the hospital. How much time was left for me?

"Mr. Henshel?" the receptionist said. "You can go in now. Room Seven."

The man in the suit stood up. He was the patient after all. I knew a wig when I saw one.

"And Kim Smith," the receptionist went on, "the nurse is ready to draw some blood."

"Interview with a vampire," Kim muttered. She winked at me, but I was too numb to wink back.

Kim edged past me on her way out to the hall. "Tell them about Sister Euphrasia," she whispered.

I shook my head. Mom and Dad would never run to a faith healer. We'd gone over it a dozen times with my cousin Rena.

"Try," Kim whispered. "Don't give up."

34

"I don't even know where she lives," I whispered back.

"New Orleans," Kim said close to my ear. "The French Quarter."

"Shannon," Dad called. "Let's go."

"Bye," I told Kim. "Thanks."

On my way out of the waiting room, I noticed Jonathan looking at me. I thought he shook his head no, but I couldn't be certain.

4

I'm not sure when I first thought of running away. Maybe the idea came to me when I saw my cousin Rena.

Rena dropped by the next afternoon with a bunch of jars from the health-food store. Eagerly she spread them on the kitchen table — wheat germ, ginseng, vitamins, garlic capsules. I offered her a snack, but she turned down everything except a carrot and some celery stalks.

Rena had just finished college and gotten her own apartment. She was a potter. She made cups and bowls and vases, and sold them at crafts fairs all over Wisconsin. Dad said she didn't make much money at it — that's why she lived on rabbit food. But it wasn't just lack of funds. Rena sincerely believed in vegetables.

"You look great," she told me as I put the vitamins in the cupboard. "How do you feel, now that you're off all those drugs?"

"I'm *not* off them," I said grimly. "They're putting me back on again."

Mom came in as I was telling the whole gruesome story. "Is this true, Aunt Peggy?" Rena demanded. "After everything she's been through?"

"We've made a decision," Mom said firmly. "It wasn't easy, believe me. We're doing what we think is best."

There was nothing to say to that, and Rena let the subject go. But as soon as Mom was gone again, she seized her chance. "If I were you," she said, "I'd take a stand on this treatment thing."

"I'm only fourteen," I reminded her. "I'm a minor. How can I refuse?"

Rena took another crunchy bite of celery. "I don't know," she said. "There's got to be a way."

She couldn't find one, though. She thought and thought, sitting there at the kitchen table, and got nowhere. When she finally left, she just squeezed my hand and told me to eat plenty of garlic.

Still, Rena made me turn things over in my mind. Suppose I simply refused to go into the hospital. What could they do about it?

They could take me there by force, kicking and crying. I'd feel mean and childish, throwing a tantrum like that! In the end I'd probably give up in shame.

But suppose I suggested an alternative to Dr.

Calder's treatment. Suppose I asked Dad and Mom to let me try something else instead. Something with scientific backing, something that had worked for hundreds of other people with cancer. Maybe I could persuade them to take me for a visit to Sister Euphrasia.

No, that idea was a dead end, too. Dad had no patience with "snake-oil sellers," as he called them. As far as he was concerned, all faith healers belonged behind bars. I might have had a fighting chance if I could have given them a real name, first, middle, and last. Better yet, he would have liked a name followed by official-sounding letters — M.A., Ph.D. I couldn't seriously ask to go see someone named Sister Euphrasia.

In the meantime, Mom marked the calendar. My first evaluation appointment was scheduled for July 23. Evaluation meant that they stuck me with a monster needle and removed about a gallon of my blood. (The guy in the lab coat said it was only a half pint, but what did he know?) My second evaluation, which was more of the same, was set for July 30. There was a red circle around Thursday, August 2. That was the day I would be readmitted to the hospital.

I felt well, better than I had in three years. At last my body was free from the chemicals that had driven the cancer away. I was no longer plagued with headaches and weakness, nausea and canker sores. I woke each morning strong and rested. The world awaited, with a thousand possibilities.

These summer days should have been joyful and carefree, a glorious reward. I'd earned them, hadn't I? For years I'd been a good, cooperative patient. I'd done whatever was required, with the hope that someday I would be well.

But the reward had been snatched away from me. The hospital loomed before me once more.

The last days of July were heavy with heat. Sometimes Abby and I escaped to the pool. Other days we hung out talking and playing video games. Dad rigged up a hammock between two trees in the backyard, and after supper I'd lie there and read until the mosquitoes drove me inside. I hated saying good-bye to another day. It meant that the big red circle on the calendar crept a little bit closer.

One morning Mom called to me from the dining room, where she was sorting through the mail. "There's an important-looking envelope for you," she said. "Looks like something you've been waiting for."

For a moment I had no idea what she was talking about. Then I saw the return address: Wisconsin Arts Foundation.

All that fuss over the drawing contest seemed so long ago. The article from the paper was still stuck to the refrigerator, but by now it was partly covered by notes and reminders. I'd almost forgotten there was anything more to come. I had won a prize.

Carefully, I tore open the envelope. There it was, a check written to me, Shannon Thomas. The amount was clear and unmistakable: five hundred dollars.

In the history of the world, this was the first time that a check in that amount had ever been written to me. I knew that I should be thrilled. But I felt nothing. It was only a slip of paper with numbers on it.

I didn't need money. Sure, I could buy CD's, posters, new clothes for starting school. But none of those things really mattered. Money couldn't keep the cancer away. It couldn't spare me from more chemotherapy.

"What are you going to do with your newfound wealth?" Dad asked later, when he came home from work. I shook my head and said I didn't know. But somewhere in my mind, an idea had taken root. Surely five hundred dollars was more than enough for a ticket to New Orleans.

"Well," Dad said, "for safekeeping, you'd better stash it in the bank. You can always take it out when you make up your mind."

I glanced at him in surprise. I thought he'd want me to do something boring and responsible, like tuck the money into my college account. Maybe Dad was thinking of that five-year limit Dr. O'Brien had explained to us. I might not be around long enough to go to college. I'd be wise to spend my money now, while I had the chance to enjoy it.

"Okay," I said. "Let's go to the bank tomorrow. Only I don't want to deposit the check. I want to cash it."

"You shouldn't keep that kind of money around the house," Dad exclaimed, as I knew he would.

"It's not like anyone's going to break in and steal it," I pointed out. "I just want to have it here, where I can get it if I want to buy something special."

One thing I'd learned over the past three years — parents have a hard time saying no to a kid with cancer. Dad frowned and grumbled about the interest I'd be losing. But in the end I won the argument. Early the next morning, before he set out for work, Dad drove me to the bank. The teller counted ten crisp fifty-dollar bills into my hand.

"Don't keep it all in one place," Dad warned as he dropped me off at the house. "That way, if anything happens, you won't lose all of it."

"I'll be careful," I promised. I patted my purse, knowing the money was safely folded inside.

"You know what you're going to do yet?" Dad

asked as I opened the car door. "Figured out what you want to spend it on?"

"I'm still thinking," I said. "I'm getting an idea."

Mom was working at home that day — telecommuting, as she called it. By ten o'clock, she was busy in her office off the living room, clicking away at her mouse. I had the house almost to myself. Still, to be sure she wouldn't overhear me, I called the airlines from the phone in the basement.

My heart raced. Thinking was one thing — gathering information was something else. I was taking a crucial step.

"Reservations and information, this is Dana, how can I help you?" said a brisk female voice.

For a moment I couldn't speak. I opened my mouth, but no sound came out.

"Reservations and information," Dana began again.

"How much does it cost to fly from here to New Orleans?" I gasped.

"What is your departure point, ma'am?" Dana asked politely.

"My what?"

"Where will you be departing from?"

"Oh. I'm in Madison. Madison, Wisconsin. That's the state capital," I added. Now that I'd found my voice, I couldn't seem to turn it off again.

"We have no direct flights from Madison, Wisconsin, to New Orleans, Louisiana," Dana said. "You'll have to change planes in Chicago."

"What's the cheapest flight I can get?"

There was a long silence. I waited for Dana to bring up the details on her computer screen. Through the ceiling I heard Mom's footsteps. She had left her office and was crossing the kitchen. What would I say if she came downstairs and found me making this call? My heart thudded harder. Hurry up, Dana! I thought. Come on!

"If you leave on a weekday and stay over a Saturday night, giving fourteen days advance notice, your round-trip fare will be two fifty-nine plus tax," she said into my ear.

Two fifty-nine! It sounded like an awful lot. But it was just a little more than half of my five hundred dollars. I'd still have plenty left for other things I needed. I'd have to buy food. And I didn't know how much Sister Euphrasia charged . . .

Then I absorbed the rest of Dana's words. I was due to go into the hospital next Thursday. That was only one week away now. "Fourteen days notice?" I asked. "You mean, like I've got to sign up two weeks ahead of time?"

"That is correct," Dana said. "If you make your reservation less than fourteen days before your scheduled departure date, the round-trip fare will be three sixty-eight."

More than a hundred dollars more. Still, I'd have enough. I could manage.

"Okay," I said. "Can you put my name down?"

"How do you care to purchase your ticket?" Dana inquired. "Can you give me a credit card number, please?"

From upstairs, I heard Mom running water in the sink. I hoped the noise would keep my voice from filtering up to her. "I haven't got a credit card," I said, almost in a whisper. "Can you just put my name down, and I'll give you the money when I — if I — "

"All tickets must be prepaid," Dana said sternly. "We can only accept a credit card, check, or money order."

"But I've got the money!" I protested. "I can pay in cash!"

"Listen," Dana said, and her voice was kinder. "How old are you, honey?"

"I'm fourteen," I said. I felt as though I were confessing a crime.

"And you'll be flying alone?"

"Yeah. It's just me."

"Well," Dana said, "in order for you to board, you need your parents' written permission."

The door opened at the top of the stairs. "Shannon?" Mom called. "Are you down there?"

"Right here," I called back. "I've got to go," I said into the phone, my words hushed and urgent. "Thanks a lot, okay? Bye!"

"Why are you using the phone down here?" Mom asked, descending the first few steps.

"It's cooler in the basement," I said. It was the only excuse I could think of. It popped out before I could weigh it carefully.

"I put the air conditioner on an hour ago," Mom said. "It's not bad up here."

"I forgot," I said. It was a pretty poor lie. But I was only starting out. That morning I couldn't guess how good I'd become at rearranging the truth.

5

Without any further questions, Mom shut herself into her office again. I went up to my room and threw myself across my bed. It had been crazy to think I could run off by myself and see Sister Euphrasia. The last time I took a Madison city bus alone, I'd gotten on the wrong one. How could I possibly find my way to New Orleans?

I wasn't going anywhere. If I were older — seventeen or eighteen maybe — I could figure out what to do. But I was just a kid. What did I know about dealing with the world? I couldn't even buy an airline ticket.

I sat up and put on a CD. As the music flooded the room, I realized that I felt relieved. It was terrifying to think of sneaking away from the house and setting off into the unknown. Now I knew I couldn't go. I would stay home. Where I felt safe. Where I knew what to expect.

I knew what to expect, all right. Soon I'd be flat

on my back in a hospital bed, calling a nurse to bring me a basin.

It wasn't fair! I'd gone through my trial by fire. I'd put it all behind me. No one had the right to make me go back!

Why didn't anybody listen when I explained how I felt? Why wasn't I allowed to speak when they made decisions about my life? Why did I go along with those decisions so meekly, as if I had no choice?

All right, I thought, I couldn't buy a plane ticket to New Orleans. But I still had my five hundred dollars. There had to be another way.

I was starting to learn the rules of deception. I left the CD player on so Mom would assume I was still in my room. Then I sneaked back to the basement to make some more phone calls.

The bus company was a lot more casual than the airlines about minors traveling alone. I didn't mention my age when I called, and nobody asked. I wouldn't need a credit card — or a reservation, for that matter. If I showed up at the station on time, and if I had the cash in hand, I could climb aboard the bus. I'd have to make a lot of stops and changes along the way. It sounded pretty tricky. But the buses could get me to New Orleans, if I managed to take the right ones.

When I hung up the phone, I felt giddy. I could do it! I could pay my fare, take those buses, and find Sister Euphrasia! Not even Dr. O'Brien had promised me a cure. Wait and see, that was the best she could offer. If you live five years, then you're safe. But Sister Euphrasia touched sick people and made them well. All those scientists couldn't be wrong, could they? She had the gift, Kim said. Some people have it, nobody knows why . . .

Shakily I mounted the stairs and pulled out a chair in the kitchen. Nothing was simple and clear-cut anymore. I *did* have a choice. A decision lay before me, and I had to work it out on my own.

I tried to imagine the journey step-by-step. I'd pack an overnight bag. I'd study a map of the city buses, and figure out how to reach the Greyhound station. I'd choose a time when Mom and Dad were out of the house. Once I got to the station, I'd buy my ticket, take a seat, and watch the scenery slide past the windows.

How many hours would the trip last? I hadn't thought to ask. I wasn't even sure how far New Orleans was from Madison. And once I arrived, how would I find Sister Euphrasia? The French Quarter, Kim said. What in the world was a French Quarter? It sounded like a foreign coin.

If I was going to look for Sister Euphrasia, I had to have her address. I couldn't count on running into Kim at my next appointment. I'd have to call her up. And I didn't even know her number. I returned to the basement and called Dr. Calder's office.

"Hi," I said when the receptionist answered. "This is Shannon Thomas. I have a question. I was wondering — "

"Are you a patient here?" the receptionist asked. She still didn't remember my name!

"Yes," I said. "I'm kind of new. There's another patient I met there, a girl. She's about fifteen. Kim Smith. I want to get in touch with her."

"I'm sorry, we can't give out telephone numbers," the receptionist said. "It's against our policy."

"Please? I know she wouldn't mind!"

"I'm afraid not," the receptionist said. "If you want, I can give her a note from you."

"Never mind," I said. "I'll just look in the phone book."

The receptionist gave a short laugh. "Okay," she said. "Good luck!"

Back in the kitchen, I dragged out the Madison phone directory. The receptionist had a very weird sense of humor. There were nineteen columns of Smiths. Each column had nearly one hundred names.

I was spared after all. There was no decision to make. I could never get Sister Euphrasia's address in time.

I'd been playing a game with myself, pretending I could escape the hospital. But I couldn't run away. The IV bags, the nausea, the utter helplessness were inevitable. Lying there in my bed between cold steel rails, I would remind myself that at least I had tried to find a way out. But no, I'd be too sick to remember. The hours would melt together, and time would lose its meaning. Night and morning would all be the same, the same clammy fog of misery.

I glanced at the calendar. We were still on the July page. Under the 30th, Mom had written one of her quick coded messages: "Shan eval appt." *Shannon's evaluation appointment*. Gingerly I lifted the page to look at August. There it was, that big red circle. Thursday, August 2: "Shan hosp." *Shannon hospital*.

I turned away, letting the page fall back into place. One week more! A week was such a tiny sliver of time between me and the months of torture. And then, when it was all over, there was still no assurance that the treatment would work. No one could swear that the cancer was gone forever. I would spend the next five years worrying that every pimple or twinge or fever was a sign of doom.

"I'm going for a walk," I called to Mom, and banged out the back door into a burst of midday heat. The birds were silent, and the trees drooped as though the air weighed them down. It was no day for walking. But I couldn't sit in the house a moment longer.

No one was out on the sidewalk. I had the streets all to myself. I wandered aimlessly, watching the pavement. I hardly noticed where I went. A phrase found its way into my head, and played itself over and over. *Between a rock and a hard place.* I'd never understood what that meant before. Now I knew. There was the hospital, the rock, waiting to crush me. It offered hope in the form of statistics, percentages, a jumble of odds. I knew the odds game, and it didn't seem to work in my favor.

Then there was New Orleans, the hard place, a place I'd never seen and could scarcely imagine. It was a place full of confusion, maybe even danger, where I would search desperately for a mysterious woman I had never met.

But New Orleans offered something the hospital could never promise. Sister Euphrasia was a healer. She touched people and they were cured.

Ever since they told me I had Hodgkin's disease, people had urged me to go ahead and lead a normal life. But my life could never be normal. How could I plan for a future that was speckled with question marks? College, a career, a family — I might not have time for any of those things that other people took for granted.

If Sister Euphrasia was really famous, people in

New Orleans would know who she was. Even without an address, I could find her. Perhaps she could end my uncertainty. Perhaps she could give me back my future.

I looked up and saw the spiraling form of a jungle gym. As if they had a will of their own, my feet had carried me to the park. A couple of little girls were busy on the swings, but the jungle gym stood deserted. I remembered Virginia, perched high and defiant, daring me to come after her. For a second I gazed at the top bar where she had sat. Again I recalled my sense of helplessness and frustration. Virginia, one little five-year-old, had more control over her life than I had over mine.

I grabbed a crossbar and scrambled upward.

The sun made the steel bars hot to the touch, but I kept climbing. At the peak I twisted around and sat, swinging my feet in the air. From a nearby tree, a squirrel eyed me suspiciously. It was glorious to look down from this height. No wonder Virginia had known such a sense of power. It was only a set of monkey bars, but up here I felt strong, confident, unstoppable. I was mistress of my own fate.

No one else could make my decisions. Nobody else knew what was best for me. I had the right to choose, and before me lay two possibilities.

My future rested between a rock and a hard

place. Suddenly, from the top of the jungle gym, my course was clear. I didn't have her address or even her full name. But I would search for Sister Euphrasia. The hard place was the choice I had to make.

6

There's something exciting about being afraid. That night at supper, I fought against wave after wave of terror. I stared at my plate, unable to eat until Mom asked if I felt all right.

"I'm fine," I said, and somehow I really was. I felt strong and bold and ready for anything.

"You look a little flushed," Mom said, with worry in her voice. Frowning, she put a cool hand to my forehead. "You don't feel like you've got a temperature," she conceded. "Try to eat your chicken, okay?"

"What did you do all day?" Dad asked, changing the subject.

"Nothing much," I said. "Just hung around."

"Didn't Abby come over?"

"No, she had to go to her grandmother's. I'll see her tomorrow."

They were always concerned about me. I was an only child with a life-threatening disease. Mom and Dad checked up on me constantly, as though they thought any minute I might stop breathing.

They'd be frantic when they discovered I had run away. I'd leave them a note, of course. I'd assure them that I was safe and would be back soon. But they wouldn't believe it. They'd phone everybody they knew, trying to figure out where I might have gone. Maybe they'd even call the police. I wished I could spare them all that distress. But if I asked them to take me to Sister Euphrasia, they'd refuse. Dad would lecture me about getting taken in by cheats and quacks. He'd go on and on about facing tough realities. Realities like more chemotherapy.

I picked at my chicken without tasting it. When could I get away? Mom would be home tomorrow, and they'd both be around all weekend. Monday was "Shan eval appt." That left only Tuesday and Wednesday. It was cutting it awfully close.

Once in a while help comes exactly when you need it. Mom and I were in the kitchen, slicing peaches for dessert, when the phone rang. Mom picked it up. From the tone of her voice, I knew it was Aunt Kath.

"Heat?" Mom said, laughing. "What heat? We're basking in our air-conditioning. Enjoying all the comforts of technology." She paused, listening. "I bet it is. Don't make me envious!"

Aunt Kath wasn't my real aunt. She was Mom's roommate in college, and they'd stayed friends all these years. Every summer Aunt Kath and some of her friends rented a house in Door County on Lake Michigan, which was why Mom was so full of envy.

"Tomorrow?" Mom exclaimed. "What do you mean, would we like to? Sure, I can get time off. I'll work Saturday to make it up." She turned to me. "Shannon, you want to spend a day out at Aunt Kath's place?"

"Okay," I said. Then I caught myself. Fate had handed me the opportunity I needed. "Tomorrow?" I asked, trying to sound dismayed. "I'm going to the mall with Abby tomorrow!"

"Wouldn't you rather go to the lake instead? You can go to the mall any day."

I thought fast. "I haven't seen Abby all week," I said. "She'd be disappointed."

"I don't know about Shannon," Mom said into the phone. "She's got some plan with her friend. But *I'll* be out there. Can I bring anything for lunch?"

My legs began to tremble. They shook so hard I could barely stand. I thought Mom would ask me what was wrong, but she was engrossed in a serious discussion about potato salad. I staggered up to my room and sank onto the bed, shivering. Tomorrow Mom would be with Aunt Kath all day. Dad would be at work. I could get away.

This wasn't my own voice I heard in my head. It couldn't be me, Shannon Thomas, making these wild plans. Shannon Thomas was a mouse. She was afraid of the kids at school, afraid of the teachers, afraid of little Virginia! How could Shannon Thomas find her way to the bus station? How could she manage all those complicated changes — in Chicago, St. Louis, Little Rock? What would she do on the streets of New Orleans, searching for Sister Euphrasia? Alone.

Nothing felt real. It was as though I were watching a video, waiting to see what would happen. I had turned the machine on, and now the credits were rolling. Pretty soon I would view the opening scene of *On the Run*.

That night I couldn't sleep. Finally, at four in the morning, I stumbled out of bed and pulled my backpack from the closet. It was tan, made of sturdy canvas, with lots of handy zipper compartments inside and out. I hadn't used it since Abby's sleepover birthday party, back in May.

What was I going to need? I'd be heading south — the weather would be hot. Shorts, a couple of tank tops, and a sweater, in case the bus was air-conditioned. Underwear. My comb and brush. Some books to read on the way. A sketch pad and pencils — I might have a long wait somewhere . . .

Carefully I gathered each item, crossing it off my mental checklist. My backpack began to bulge. I picked it up and slung it over my shoulder. It was heavier that I expected, but not bad. I could manage.

How long would I be gone? With all those layovers and changes, the trip might take a whole day. And then, who knew how much time I'd have to spend tracking down Sister Euphrasia? I could be gone three days.

Three days wasn't such a long time, I reminded myself. But Mom and Dad wouldn't see it that way. Maybe I could call them from a phone booth somewhere and tell them I was all right. No, they'd be so mad I'd be afraid to talk to them. I'd send them a message somehow. I'd think of a way. On that long bus ride I'd have plenty of time to think!

I was forgetting something! I tiptoed into the bathroom and grabbed my toothbrush and toothpaste. I'd never hear the end of it if I went off without them! I was tucking them into a zipper compartment when the weirdness of it struck me, and I almost laughed out loud. I pictured myself coming home after my long journey, face-to-face with Mom and Dad at last, saying, "But I did remember to brush my teeth!"

I should have been yawning over breakfast, but I felt wide-awake. It was almost an ordinary morning. Dad and Mom passed sections of the paper back and forth across the table. Mom turned the radio to the classical station, and the strains of a violin filled the kitchen. The sights and sounds around me were only background to the plans that raced through my mind. As soon as Mom and Dad were gone, I would go into action.

"Are you positive you don't want to come up to Aunt Kath's?" Mom asked as I poured myself another glass of orange juice.

"I'm meeting Abby at eleven," I said. "We're going out to that new mall, you know? The one with The Gap." If I were Pinocchio, my nose would have grown three inches.

"I don't see what's the big attraction about shopping," Dad remarked. "On my list it's down around dentist appointments and car inspection."

"I guess you just can't relate," Mom said. "You were never a fourteen-year-old girl."

"No," Dad said, reaching for the sports page. "I never was. You're absolutely right."

I couldn't do anything until they both left, and for a while it looked as though they would never go. Dad worked in one of the big office buildings next to the State Capitol. Usually he left by ten after eight, taking the bus to avoid the hassle of downtown parking. But today he sat longer and longer over his second cup of coffee, lost in a newspaper article. It was nearly eight-thirty when he finally pushed back his chair. "I'd better drive," he said. "Otherwise I'll never make it on time!"

Once he was out the door, Mom puttered around clearing the table and stacking the dishwasher. "I can do that," I told her. "Don't you need to get going?"

"I've got plenty of time," Mom assured me. "I told Aunt Kath I'd be up there sometime before noon."

"But don't you want to get an early start?" I asked hopefully.

For a second Mom glanced my way, her eyes narrowed. "What's the matter — are you trying to get rid of me?" she asked with a short laugh.

Suddenly I was on the alert. "No, of course not," I said quickly. "I just thought you'd want to get up there as soon as you can, so you can enjoy a full day."

"Don't worry," she said. "I will."

So I waited. I waited while she made phone calls from her office. I waited while she went to the basement with a basket of laundry. I waited while she watered the spider plant in the dining-room window. And at last, at *last*, she climbed into the car and pulled out of the driveway. "Good-bye!" I called from the porch, waving wildly.

"Be good," Mom called back, and her words pierced straight through me. I couldn't look at her as I shouted a last farewell.

When I stepped back inside, the silence engulfed me. My footsteps echoed across the kitchen floor. I was on my own now. I could do whatever I chose, and no one would stop me.

On a bookcase in the living room, I found Dad's map of the city bus system. I would only have to take one bus to reach the Greyhound station; it wouldn't be hard, even for me. On impulse, I pulled a heavy atlas down from a shelf and flipped to a map of the United States. My finger traced the route I would follow — from Madison to Chicago, on to St. Louis, Little Rock, and New Orleans at last. I would cover more than a thousand miles on my journey, from the country's northern rim to the Gulf Coast.

What would Abby think when I didn't show up for our trip to the mall? I wanted to rush to the phone and tell her everything. But I stopped myself in time. Mom and Dad would talk to Abby as soon as they realized I was missing. If she knew anything, she would have to share it with them. I couldn't take the chance. I couldn't reveal my plans to anyone.

Upstairs, I reached into the back of my top bureau drawer. My fingers closed on the envelope with my money from the Arts Foundation. Standing in the light from the window, I counted out the fat bundle of bills. Five hundred dollars! Surely it was enough to take me to New Orleans and bring me home again. I'd probably have a couple hundred dollars to spare.

The money made my wallet so thick that it hardly fit into my pocketbook. Maybe Dad was right. It wasn't a good idea to keep all my cash in one place. I counted out two fifty-dollar bills and slipped them into a pocket of my backpack. I felt a surge of pride at my cleverness. Even if disaster struck and I lost my pocketbook, I wouldn't be penniless. I'd have enough money to see me through.

Back in the kitchen, I set my bags on the table. I dreaded this final moment, but I couldn't avoid it any longer. I found a pen by the phone and wrote a note on Mom's message pad, where she was sure to see it.

Dear Mom and Dad,

Please don't worry about me. I can't tell you where I've gone, but I'll be back soon. I am perfectly safe. I have thought this out carefully, and it is the best thing for me to do. When I get home I will explain everything.

I love you always.

Shannon

I read the note once, and added a quick postscript. "Please don't be mad at Abby," I wrote. "She wasn't in on this at all. She doesn't even know about it."

I stepped onto the porch and pulled the door shut behind me. On the sidewalk I stopped for one long, backward glance. By the time I saw this familiar redbrick house again, I could be cured. I could be free to live my life without "ifs" and "maybes." I would be someone I didn't know yet, somebody brand-new.

"Good-bye," I said out loud, and started up the street to the bus stop.

7

"I want to buy a bus ticket." This couldn't be me, standing in the Greyhound station with my pocketbook and my backpack. I didn't recognize my voice saying those strange words to the woman behind the counter. This was the new Shannon Thomas.

"Where are you going?" the woman asked, raising her eyebrows.

Didn't she understand what I had achieved this morning? I'd found my way to the Greyhound station all by myself, without getting lost once.

"You want a ticket to where?" the woman asked. She was called Jessica Tinley, according to her nametag. She was not much older than my cousin Rena. Her hair was such a glossy blonde that I knew it wasn't her natural color. She looked at me carefully, her forehead puckered in a frown. Maybe the bus people *did* care how old their passengers were, after all.

"I'm going to ..." I hesitated. New Orleans was so far away! Jessica Tinley would really be suspicious if she heard that one! "I'm going to Chicago," I told her, pulling out my wallet. "To see my aunt."

For a long moment she looked me up and down. Behind me in line, a couple of college kids grumbled impatiently. "How old are you?" the ticket woman asked bluntly.

"Sixteen," I said. It was much easier to lie now. Practice made a tremendous difference.

"Where's your driver's license?" Ms. Tinley demanded.

My heart tumbled to the pit of my stomach. In another second, she would reach for the phone. She'd call the police, the juvenile court, whoever people called in a case like this. *All points alert! Runaway kid on the loose!*

"I haven't got a license," I heard my strange new voice explain. "If I had my driver's license, do you think I'd be taking the bus?"

Behind me, the college kids tittered. Jessica Tinley seemed to notice them for the first time. Beyond them, the line snaked back toward the door. It grew longer by the minute.

With a last, disapproving frown, the ticket agent made her decision. "Chicago leaves at ten forty-five," she said. "Platform Seventeen."

Relief swept over me like a great, billowing

breeze. I handed over my money and turned away, folding the change back into my wallet. I had no idea where Platform Seventeen might be, but I set off at a trot.

I had just spotted a sign that said PLAT-FORMS 15-22, when I heard a shout. "Hey! You forgot your ticket!"

I glanced back, aghast. Ms. Tinley waved at me above the heads of the waiting hordes. She held up a small white envelope.

I felt like myself again, slinking back to the counter. The real Shannon Thomas had returned, bungling her way through life. I cowered before the ticket agent, ready to make a full confession. I'm not old enough for a driver's license, I'd tell her. And when the police get here, I won't even be able to tell them where I live, because I'm so scared I don't think I can remember . . .

"Hang on to this," Ms. Tinley said. She slipped the envelope into my hand. "You're boarding in twenty minutes. You've still got time."

For a long second I stood frozen. She didn't snatch up the phone. No one was coming to claim me after all. I was dismissed.

"Thank you!" I called over my shoulder. I wanted to break into a run, but my legs were so wobbly I could barely stand upright. Following the arrow, I half staggered out to Platform Seventeen.

The waiting area was a bleak, hollow room with rows of molded plastic chairs bolted to the floor. The music that dripped from the overhead speaker reminded me of Dr. Calder's office. I thought of Kim Smith. What would she say if she could see me now? I'd have some incredible stories to tell her the next time we met.

But I might never run into Kim again. I might never have to go back to Dr. Calder. Sister Euphrasia would draw every last trace of cancer from my body. I would be cured, free to live my life like anyone else.

I settled onto one of the plastic seats and studied the faces around me. Three elderly women clustered together, laughing over some private joke. A bearded man listened to a Walkman, his foot tapping to a beat no one else could hear. Across from me, a woman bounced a baby on her lap. The baby was beautiful, with sparkling dark eyes and a full head of black hair. I dug into my backpack and pulled out a sketch-pad. On this strange, unreal day, it was comforting to hold a pencil in my fingers, to make a picture grow on the page before me.

"Joey, get over here now!"

I looked up guiltily, as if I were the one being scolded. Joey's mother stood in the doorway of the waiting room. She towed two identical little boys, one by each hand — twin redheads in denim jeans. As I looked on, Joey skidded into view. He was nine or ten, with thick wire-rimmed glasses.

"Stick with us!" his mother told him. "I've got enough to do without hunting for you every five minutes!"

"Can I buy a CD?" Joey asked. "There's a place out there that sells them."

"Sit down!" his mother said, glaring. "Jacob, Jason, all of you, sit down and give me a break!"

I've always been fascinated by big families. Maybe it comes from being an only child. To me, a family is big if it has more than one kid in it. This one had three, and they were all moving so fast they looked like twice that many. Jacob and Jason, the twins, stayed in their seats for about three seconds. Then they slid to the floor in a noisy wrestling match. Joey danced around them, cheering them on. Their mother abandoned all hope of getting them to sit still. She just wanted to be sure the twins didn't damage each other.

"Hey, may I see that?"

It was the woman with the baby. She was craning to get an upside-down look at my sketch.

Hot color spread up my cheeks. I hadn't meant to attract attention. I just wanted to draw in peace.

"Okay," I said cautiously. I passed her the pad.

"That looks just like him," she said, breaking into a warm smile. "Do you take art lessons?"

"On and off," I said. I had to drop out of class every time I went into the hospital for more chemo.

"Well, you should stay with it," she said, handing back the sketch-pad. "You have a lot of talent."

"Thank you," I said, and felt the flush creep a little higher.

"Are you by yourself?" she asked.

I couldn't lie to her. She was too nice. But I sensed I shouldn't tell her anything close to the truth. I decided to ignore the question, as if I hadn't heard it. "Here," I said, tearing off the baby's picture. "You can keep it if you want."

"Oh, that's lovely!" she exclaimed, taking it back. "Thank you so much!"

Just then a rough, metallic voice broke through the piped-in music. "All passengers for Chicago, Des Moines, Omaha, and Denver! Your bus is now boarding at Platform Seventeen!"

Sure enough, our bus waited outside, grunting and puffing. We all scrambled to our feet. I checked my pocket. There was the envelope with my ticket, crisp and reassuring to my touch. I hoisted my backpack and moved toward the door with the rest of the crowd.

Joey and his family were in front of me. One of the twins burst into song, something about losing your underwear. "Jacob, please!" his mother protested. I wondered how she could tell which twin was which.

I stepped outside. By now the sun blazed down.

Acrid diesel fumes hung heavy in the air. I followed Joey's family to the bus and stood in line to clamber aboard. The bearded man with the Walkman edged up beside me. "You lost?" he asked. "Need some help?"

Maybe he was trying to be pleasant. Probably he wasn't the least bit dangerous. I'd been watching too many horror movies, reading too many Stephen King books.

But all my life my parents had warned me against talking to strangers. The very worst kind were strange men.

"Can I help you in any way?" the man with the Walkman persisted.

I shook my head and inched closer to Joey's family. I felt safer being near a mother. Anybody's mother would do, if I couldn't have mine.

By the time Jacob and Jason bounded up the steps of the bus, I had maneuvered in right behind them. I watched their mother hand the driver their tickets, and saw what I was supposed to do. When it was my turn, the driver cast a curious, worried glance toward me. I didn't say a word. I just pointed toward Joey and the others, as if to say we were all together. I hoped that the bearded man would believe me.

Joey and the others never seemed to notice me. Calmly, purposefully, I followed them down the bus's narrow aisle. They spent a lot of time putting bags into the overhead rack, then pulling them down again to find Legos and action figures. When they were settled at last, I took a seat in the row behind them. I had adopted a family. For this leg of the journey, at least, I was not alone.

8

For a little while, the bus rolled through the familiar streets of Madison. But soon we left the city behind. Cornfields and pastures opened out on either side of the highway. We passed grazing herds of brown and white dairy cows. Now and then I glimpsed a horse, its head lifted to gaze at the endless stream of traffic.

On long drives when I was little, I used to count the cows and horses along the road. Whenever we drove through a patch of woods, I'd keep on the lookout for deer. Counting the animals helped me stave off boredom. Today I tried that old trick again. I began to count: forty-three cows, twelve horses, six goats, even a llama. I wasn't bored this time. Counting was a way to keep the world in order. It helped me not to feel afraid.

At first Joey and his brothers kept busy with hand-held video games. Then the twins built a Lego castle, laying a cardboard box lid on the seat between them. Joey leaned over them, making unwelcome suggestions. The twins kept pleading to their mother, "Make him quit it! Make him stop bothering us!"

"Try to get along," she advised, but it was a lost cause. Finally she gave Joey a no-nonsense glare and said, "Leave your brothers alone!"

After that, the row in front of me was quieter, and much less interesting. For a time, Joey and the twins had pushed my worries aside. Now they swarmed back to overwhelm me.

Dad would be the first one home tonight. He wouldn't be concerned over the empty house. He'd assume I was still shopping with Abby. He'd head for the living room and switch on the news, and wouldn't see my note on the pad by the phone.

Mom would get home later. She'd come in, sunburned and happy, ready to tell us Aunt Kath's latest adventures. And I would not be there.

"Where's Shannon?" she'd ask Dad. "She ought to be home by now. Didn't she call?"

They'd wait a little longer, and then Mom would decide to phone Abby's house. She'd have to look up the number in the Rolodex. She would spot my note as she stood by the kitchen counter. She'd call Dad, and read it to him out loud, and they would both go into panic.

I didn't want to picture what would surely come next: the two of them making desperate phone calls, jumping in the car to search the neighborhood, sitting up all night with the porch light on just in case . . .

Hastily I looked out the window. Five cows stood in the field we were passing. And up ahead I counted seven more.

It wasn't long, though, before a sign announced, "Welcome to Illinois." Soon farmland melted into suburban developments. Chicago loomed closer and closer. Forty-eight miles, according to one sign. Twenty-seven . . . sixteen . . .

"We're almost there," said Joey's mother. "Put your things away."

Then one of the twins discovered that he had lost a plastic T-rex. He was working up to some serious crying when I spied it on the floor at my feet.

I bent down and picked it up. Its mouth bristled with purple teeth. "Here you go," I said, handing it to him over the back of his seat.

"Thank you," said my adopted mother from across the aisle. "You saved the day!"

"No, *you* did," I said. Joey was lobbying for lunch at McDonald's, and I knew she wouldn't hear me.

"Chicago!" our driver called out. "Change here for all destinations!"

It was one forty-five by my watch. I was three long hours away from Madison, Wisconsin, away from everything I had known all my life. Clambering down the high steps from the bus, I knew that in those few hours I had crossed into a different world.

The Greyhound station was a sad place. Tattered, tired-looking people hovered around a dreary lunch stand. I thought I was hungry until I saw the plastic-wrapped sandwiches and dry, ancient slices of cake. The soda machine ate two of my quarters and refused to give me anything. I jiggled the lever in frustration, trying to figure out what I'd done wrong.

"That one's out of order," said a voice behind me. "Try the one over here."

I turned to see a slim, dark-haired boy of about sixteen. Like me, he wore a canvas backpack. His was blue instead of tan.

"Which one?" I asked.

"This one," he said. He pointed with his right hand. His left was wrapped in a thick gauze bandage.

Before I could stop him, the boy fished some change from his pocket and dropped it into the slot. "What do you want?" he asked. "A Pepsi?"

"Sure," I said, digging for a couple more quarters. When I held them out to him, he shook his head and said, "Forget it."

The can of Pepsi clattered down the chute. The boy handed it to me, smiling shyly. "Thanks," I said. He was a stranger, I reminded myself. I didn't know him. But he had an open, friendly face. I couldn't believe he was dangerous.

I took a long cool swallow of Pepsi. I hadn't realized how thirsty I was. Now I could think again. It was time to start asking questions. Where could I buy my ticket to New Orleans?

I gazed around me, searching for signs and arrows. Off to my left, people had formed a line before a booth marked INFORMATION. That was where I needed to go.

"Thanks," I told the boy.

"That's okay," he said, and I hurried away.

The line at the information booth moved slowly. Up ahead, an elderly woman handed a thick sheaf of papers through the windows. Apparently she wanted some sort of explanation, and the man in the booth was trying his best. I couldn't follow what they said, but they slid the papers back and forth, pointing and shuffling pages. Around me, people shifted and grumbled. "We'll be standing here till tomorrow morning!" muttered a gray-haired woman behind me. "We might as well camp out on the floor!"

At last the old woman gathered her papers into a disheveled bundle and walked off. The gray-haired woman heaved a loud sigh of relief. The line inched forward.

The long wait gave me time to prepare my speech. When does the next bus leave for New Orleans? I'd inquire. How much does it cost? How many changes do I have to make on the way? I'd sound totally confident, as though I made solo journeys like this every other week.

Forget you're fourteen, I told myself. Stand up nice and straight, and think seventeen at least. This time I wouldn't get flustered by questions about my driver's license. I'd have my story in place. I was on my way to college for the first time. Setting out from home on a great adventure . . .

Off to college in July? With no luggage but a backpack?

Well then, I was off on a visit. Yes, I was going to see my aunt. Aunt Mary in New Orleans. I was her favorite niece, and she had invited me down to spend a week with her. I'd never been there before, and I could hardly wait.

"So we meet again!" said a voice beside me. It was the bearded man with the Walkman. I had forgotten all about him. But here he was again, as if he were following me. He looked at me as though we were old friends, as if I belonged to him.

I sprang away from him, knocking into the gray-haired woman behind me. A fountain of Pepsi spouted from the can in my hand and spattered us both. She let out an indignant shriek, wiping at her face.

The man with the Walkman stood by, grinning. "You okay?" he asked me. "Need some help?"

"No!" I almost shouted at him. "I'm fine!"

"I was just wondering," he said. The line moved up again, and he stepped forward when I did.

The gray-haired woman glared at him. "You can't just cut in like that," she snapped. "Get to the end of the line, will you?"

"Yes, ma'am," he said with a mocking laugh. "And you have a nice day yourself." He turned back to me. "If there's anything I can do for you, just ask," he said, and took his place at the end of the line.

"Do you know him?" the gray-haired woman asked me.

I shook my head. "He just started talking to me," I explained. "I don't know his name or anything."

"I don't like the look of that guy," she said grimly. "He's a sinister character. I've got half a mind to call the cops."

For one wild instant, I almost cheered. Call the police, I wanted to tell her. Let them take him away so he'll leave me alone.

But the police would ask questions. That was part of their job. They'd have a lot of questions if they met me, a kid alone in the Chicago bus station. They'd phone Dad at work; they'd probably send me home in a squad car with the sirens blaring. I'd end up in the hospital right on schedule, and never meet Sister Euphrasia.

"No, don't call anybody!" I pleaded. "He didn't do anything wrong."

She cast me a doubtful glance. "Well," she said, "if he gives you any trouble, holler good and loud. That's usually enough to scare them off."

By now the line had crept up to the window. It was my turn next. My carefully prepared speech had deserted me. "I've got to go to New Orleans," I stammered. "Can you tell me — where's the right bus?"

The man in the window had crooked teeth and a crooked smile. His head was so bald I wondered if he'd been going through chemotherapy himself. "Going to *Norlins*, are you?" he asked. "That's a pretty long trip."

"I know," I said.

I got ready to tell him about Aunt Mary, but I didn't have to bring up her name. The information man started explaining all the connections I had to make. I listened as hard as I could, but the names and numbers tangled in my brain and I couldn't sort them out. In the end, I understood only two things clearly. My first stop would be St. Louis, Missouri. And the St. Louis bus didn't leave Chicago for two more hours.

I reached into my purse, ready to count out the money for my ticket. Just then I saw the man with the Walkman standing a few feet away. He was a sinister character, without a doubt. He wasn't in line now. He was simply watching me. He had slipped off his headset to catch every word I said.

Now he knew where I was going! Would he

board the bus for New Orleans, too? Somehow I had to lose him. I had to get away.

"I can buy my ticket later, can't I?" I asked, lowering my voice.

The information man nodded. "Right down to the wire," he assured me. "Long as you've got it when you get on board."

"Okay," I said. "Thanks."

The gray-haired woman took my place at the information booth. The Sinister Character didn't move, but he still watched me. I gazed around, searching for somewhere to hide. Suddenly I spotted a familiar figure crossing the wide concourse, a slim, dark-haired boy with a blue backpack. He was heading for the main door out to the street.

Behind me was the Sinister Character, thinking his secret, sinister thoughts. The boy from the soft drink machine was the nearest thing to a friend that I had in the whole city of Chicago. I couldn't afford to be shy.

"Wait!" I cried, and ran to catch up with him.

9

"**H**ey!" I shouted, as the boy stepped into the revolving door. "Hey, wait up!"

He didn't seem to hear me. With a swish, the door swallowed him up. He would disappear into the crowded streets of the city, and I'd never find him again. I'd be all alone.

I lunged for the door and twirled through after him. I hardly noticed the burst of heat and traffic noise outside. For a moment I didn't see him anywhere. My stomach knotted with despair. Then I caught sight of him, waiting for the light at the end of the block. My heart pounding, I raced to catch up.

"Hey!" I cried again. "Wait! Please wait!"

I slid to a panting stop beside him. He stared at me, blank with surprise.

"Oh, it's you," he said. He didn't sound friendly now. "What do you want?"

"I — I — " I couldn't begin. I didn't know what I wanted to say.

"Are you lost or something?" he demanded. "I'm the wrong guy to ask. I don't know my way around here, either."

At last I found my voice. "I'm not lost, exactly. It's just — I think there's a guy following me."

The light turned green, but the boy didn't move. "Following you?" he repeated. He glanced down the street the way I had come. A few pedestrians hurried along the sidewalk, but none of them paid me the slightest attention.

The familiar flush of embarrassment covered my face. I had to give some explanation that would make sense. "He tried to talk to me back in Madison. And now he's hanging around again."

The boy shrugged. He didn't believe me.

"The lady behind me in line didn't like him, either," I added.

"What does he look like?" The boy was finally interested.

"He's about thirty," I said. "Wiry dark hair. Maybe your height, but kind of heavy. And he's got a Walkman and a beard."

"Did he threaten you?" the boy asked. "Do you think he's going to kidnap you or something?"

"Maybe," I said. "He sure gave me a creepy feeling."

"You better be careful," the boy decided. "You better tell somebody."

"I *am* telling somebody!" I protested. "I'm telling *you*."

"I don't mean me," he said, backing away. "Tell that cop over there." He jerked his thumb toward a policeman patrolling the pavement in front of the bus station.

"Oh, no!" I exclaimed. "It's all right, really. Probably I just imagined the whole thing."

The boy gave me a searching look. He nodded, as though he understood at last. "Can I walk you someplace?" he asked. "Where are you going?"

"New Orleans," I blurted. I added hastily, "To see my Aunt Mary."

"Are you taking the bus or the train?"

"The train? I didn't know there *were* trains."

"I'm on my way to the Union Station," he said. "All kinds of trains come in there, going everywhere."

"Can I walk with you?" I said. I tried to get rid of the pleading note in my voice. "So I can avoid that man. In case he's back there looking for me."

The boy nodded again. We had another green light. "Sure," he said. "Come on." Together we set out across the wide street.

He said his name was Blake. I didn't ask if it was his first name or his last name. I didn't want to answer questions, so it only seemed fair not to ask any.

Without prodding, Blake told me he'd spent four hours on a bus up from Springfield, Illinois.

Now he was going to catch a train to Denver, Colorado. "It's beautiful out there," he said. "I was there when I was twelve, and I've wanted to go back ever since."

He'd only been to Chicago twice before, but he had a map of the downtown section, which he called the Loop. After we walked a block or two, he unfolded the map and plotted our course. He seemed so confident that I felt my own courage seeping back. "Look," he said, tracing the route with his forefinger. "It's not far. We're practically there already."

"I'm sure glad you know where you're going," I said. "I'd be hopelessly lost."

"Getting lost is never hopeless," he said. "You'll always find your way eventually."

"Maybe *you* will," I said, managing a laugh. "I'd probably wander in circles till I dropped."

Blake folded the map and tucked it back into his pocket. "No you wouldn't," he assured me, as we set off again. "As long as you don't panic, you can always figure out what to do."

"I was scared of getting lost when I start high school next month," I said. "Now here I am, going hundreds of miles all by myself."

I shouldn't have told him so much. Now he knew how young I really was. He'd think it was strange that I was traveling alone. What if he figured it was his civic duty to report me to the next police officer we saw?

"My parents think it's a good experience," I explained. "You know, learning to be independent."

"Are you going to tell them about the kidnapper?" Blake asked.

"I'm not sure," I said. "Really, I don't know what to tell them about anything."

"They must not get upset easily," Blake pointed out. "If they were the nervous type, they wouldn't let you do this."

He was herding me into a trap. I made a quick dodge. "They're still parents," I said. "I guess *all* parents are your basic nervous type, when you get down to it."

For a moment Blake was silent. "Not mine," he said at last. "I kind of wish they were."

An enormous building loomed ahead of us. It rose vast and imposing as a medieval fortress. As we drew nearer, I realized that this was our destination, Union Station.

Once I watched a National Geographic special about Mammoth Cave in Kentucky. The cave was a sprawling maze of caverns and tunnels, level upon level. It was an endless underground landscape, never touched by the light of the sun. Union Station reminded me a lot of Mammoth Cave. Stairways and escalators flowed up and down, from one level to the next. Signs flashed, and disembodied voices chanted arrival and departure times. I felt as though we were deep beneath the surface of the earth. In this strange, echoing world, daylight could never penetrate.

"Wow!" Blake breathed. "What do we do now?"

"There must be an information booth somewhere, like in the bus station," I suggested.

"Right," Blake said.

All around us, people were on the move — coming and going, heading out or rushing home. Only Blake and I stood still. He put his hand on my shoulder. Maybe he wanted to tell me that everything would be all right. Maybe he was trying to reassure himself.

"Over there!" I said suddenly. "It says INFORMATION and SCHEDULES. See?"

Blake looked where I pointed, and relief flashed across his face. "Let's go!" he cried, and broke into a run.

Within a few minutes we both learned something important about trains. They don't run very often. In fact, if you want to go to an out-of-the-way place like New Orleans or Denver, they only leave once a day. My train was scheduled to pull out of Chicago at 7:50 P.M. Blake's train, the one bound for Denver, had just left at three o'clock. He had missed it by thirteen minutes.

"You mean, I've got to wait till tomorrow?" he exclaimed. "I've got to hang around here for twenty-four hours?"

"Twenty-three hours and forty-seven minutes,"

the information agent corrected him. "Yup, I'm afraid that's the sad truth."

I felt sorry for Blake, but I couldn't let myself get sidetracked. "A ticket to New Orleans?" I asked. "How much is that?"

The ticket agent had a nice smile, like a teacher I had in sixth grade. "You're under fifteen, aren't you? Tell your folks you get to ride half fare."

I drew a deep breath. "My folks aren't here. I'm by myself."

The agent's smile turned to a worried frown. It was the same frown I saw whenever I stood before a window or a counter. "You're over twelve, aren't you?" he asked. "Unaccompanied minors have to be over twelve."

"I'm fourteen," I said staunchly. For the first time, being fourteen was good for something.

But it wasn't quite good enough for the ticket agent. "Do your parents know you're taking this little trip?" he inquired.

Blake edged up beside me. "Of course they know," he said. "She's going down to visit our Aunt Mary. I'm seeing her off."

"You're seeing your little sister off before you head out to Denver, is that it?" The agent sounded thoroughly skeptical.

Blake dropped his voice. "We're going through sort of a bad time at home," he said. "Dad's in Denver so I'm going out there. See, they split up, and Mom, she just needs to get herself together right now . . ."

The ticket man nodded sympathetically. "That's tough," he said. "It's always hardest on the kids." Without another word, he sold me a round-trip ticket. As we turned away from the window he called, "Good luck!"

"Thanks!" I told Blake, as soon as we were out of earshot. "I was afraid he was going to get funny."

"It's okay, Sis," Blake said, grinning. "Families gotta stick together."

By now I was starving. Blake and I found a coffee shop, and slid into a rear booth. We both ordered milkshakes and hamburgers with all the trimmings. With my first bite I started to feel better. I even felt bolder about posing questions.

"What are you going to do about Denver?" I asked. "Wait here till tomorrow?"

"I don't know," Blake said. "I better not hang around that long." He took a handful of french fries and added casually, "Somebody might be looking for me."

"Who's after you?" I asked.

For a moment I feared I had gone too far. Blake had a secret. Whatever it was, he didn't want to share it with me. I knew better than to pry.

He hesitated, gazing across the crowded coffee

shop. When he answered at last, he didn't look at me. "My old man."

"You mean, your father?" I said, bewildered.

"Yeah." Blake faced me with a thin smile. "And he's gonna kill me if he gets his hands on me!"

He had opened up a door. Perhaps he wanted to tell me after all. "How come?" I asked.

"See, it was the most incredible thing. My old man hit the lottery."

"He's a millionaire?" I gasped.

"He didn't win *that* big," Blake said quickly, holding up his hand. "He had five numbers out of the six. He got a few thousand, though — more than he ever expected to have in his life."

"Wow!" I said. "I never actually knew anybody that was a winner. It's just something you read about in the paper."

Once Blake started talking, he couldn't seem to stop. "My dad's always worked real hard," he told me. "Like he never had any fun, never bought anything special for himself. Anyway, he hit the lotto, and guess what he did. He went out and bought a brand-new Mercedes."

"My dad says if he ever won, he'd take us on a trip," I said. "He wants to see the rainforest in Brazil before it's gone."

"Well, my dad's a car freak," Blake explained. "So he gets this red Mercedes. A real beauty. His pride and joy. And I kept thinking how I'd love to get behind the wheel, just once! Just take her out for a little cruise downtown."

"Have you got your driver's license?" I asked. I could guess the answer. If he had his license, would he be taking the train?

Blake shook his head. "I'm only fifteen," he admitted. "But I figured, just one quick ride, that couldn't hurt anything, right? So last night, I kind of borrow the car keys. They're just lying there on the kitchen counter. And I take that car out and drive through the center of town, and it's so cool! And then I get the idea I'll go over and pick up my buddy, Jeff."

He paused, struggling with his thoughts. "Jeff lives out on the highway. You don't know how tricky it is, changing lanes and everything, with all that traffic coming at you from every side. You think there's nothing to it, but all of a sudden you're in the middle of it, and it's really scary!"

I saw what was coming, but I wanted to let him know I was listening. "So what happened?" I asked.

"I lost it, that's what. I just wanted to get out of there! I tried to get onto this exit ramp, and somehow — it was *so* scary! I've never been so terrified in my whole life! — somehow this Chevy station wagon plowed right into me!"

"You weren't hurt!" I said, amazed.

Blake shrugged. "Nobody was. The cops said it was a miracle. All I got were a couple of scratches." He held up his bandaged hand.

"So what'd your dad say?" I asked in awe.

"They took me down to the station and called him," Blake went on, as if he hadn't heard me. "Told him the car was totaled, and I was going to have to go to juvenile court for driving under age and all that. I didn't even dare talk to him. They said he was coming right down. I was supposed to sit in this holding area. Well, there was this nice lady keeping an eye on me, some kind of clerk I guess. She offered to go get me a Coke. And the minute her back was turned, I made a run for it," He looked down sadly at the tabletop. "I hope I didn't get her in trouble."

"What about money?" I asked. "How can you afford a train ticket?"

"I sneaked into the house real early this morning. I knew nobody'd be home. I've been working all summer for this landscaper, a friend of Dad's. I'd just gotten some money out of the bank yesterday — man, it doesn't *feel* like just yesterday! Then I headed for the bus station."

For a few minutes we were both silent. Blake pushed his plate away, almost untouched.

"Your folks must be pretty worried by now," I said cautiously.

"Mom is," Blake said. "But Dad — we don't get

91

along all that well to begin with. He'll never forgive me for this."

"Still," I said, "shouldn't you call them or something? Let them know you're all right?"

Blake shook his head. "Come on," he said. "You don't want to miss your train. Let's go find your platform."

10

My train had a name, like a ship. It was called *The City of New Orleans*. "There's a song about it!" Blake exclaimed, when we heard the boarding announcement. "My mom has it on a tape."

I didn't care whether my train had a name. I only knew that it would carry me far away. I tried to bring back the sense of urgency that drove me to leave the house this morning. But I was swept with dread. I couldn't go any farther. I had to get back to Madison. I had to go home.

"Is your aunt meeting you at the station?" Blake asked.

"What?" I said, distracted.

"Your Aunt Mary. Is she going to meet you?"

"Oh. Yeah, I guess so." Blake had told me his story. Maybe I could tell him mine.

"She's not really my aunt," I began, and stopped in confusion. I didn't know where to begin.

"Oh, I've got aunts and uncles like that, too,"

Blake said. "Just good friends of my parents."

"What I mean is . . ." I trailed off helplessly. Blake was the kind of guy who felt responsible for things. He had wanted me to tell the authorities about the man who was following me. He worried about the nice lady who let him escape from the police station. If he knew why I had bought this train ticket, he'd worry about me, too. He'd insist that I go home and take my treatment, no matter how awful it was.

"Does she live right in the city?" Blake wanted to know. "Or is she out in the suburbs?"

I tried to stall for time. I needed to think. "It's a place called the French Quarter," I said.

"Wow!" Blake said. "I've seen pictures of the French Quarter. They've got houses with these neat balconies, all this fancy wrought-iron stuff."

"Oh, boy," I said. The very last thing on my mind at that moment was architecture.

"You have to get her to take you to a seafood restaurant," Blake went on.

"Get who?"

"Your *aunt*! That's who we're talking about, isn't it?"

"Oh," I said. "Sure." People were moving through the waiting room, filing out onto the platform.

If I explained everything to Blake, he'd go back to the bus station with me. He'd stay with me until I got on the next Greyhound to Madison. I could even call Mom and Dad before I left, and assure them that I was on my way.

What was I waiting for?

"Got everything?" Blake asked.

I checked to make sure. I had my purse, backpack, a bag of corn chips, a Hershey's bar with almonds, and one round-trip ticket. "Yeah," I said. "It's all here."

If I went home, I'd have to face Mom and Dad, with all their hurt and anger. I knew how frantic they had been, how disappointed in me. I'd have to listen to hours of lectures and reproaches. They'd question me over and over, and tell me they could never trust me again. I'd have to face all that, and I would have gained nothing. I'd know I had never come close to finding Sister Euphrasia.

I wasn't brave enough to go on with my journey. But I didn't have the courage to turn back either.

I got to my feet. With Blake beside me, I crossed the platform to the waiting train. "Well, Sis," he said. "I guess it's good-bye."

I realized suddenly that he didn't even know my name. I opened my mouth to tell him, but it was too late to expain anything now. The conductor called, "Come on, young lady! Keep the line moving!"

My eyes stung with tears. I stretched out my arms and gave Blake a quick, awkward hug.

"Good-bye," I said, my voice quavering.

"Take it easy," Blake said. "Don't eat too much down there!"

"I won't," I promised.

"Bye," said Blake. He gave me a parting squeeze.

There were plenty of empty seats. I chose one by the window, which was sealed shut somehow, as though I were on a plane. Blake stood watching on the platform. I could only wave, and whisper, and hope that he could read the words on my lips. *Thank you! Good luck! Good-bye!*

The train shuddered to life. From somewhere up ahead came a long, low whistle. As we slid out of the station, I craned my neck for a last glimpse of Blake. He stood alone on the platform. He waved until we rounded a curve and he disappeared.

I curled up on the seat, my face in my hands. I pictured the steel tracks, stretching before me for hundreds of miles. They climbed hills, burrowed through tunnels, wound past cities, and leaped rivers on high, daring bridges. The train couldn't get lost. It would follow the path laid down for it, and carry me to my destination.

But I felt utterly lost, as though I'd been torn from my last friend in the world.

Scraps of conversation rattled around me. Strangers rustled through paper bags, crunched snacks, made all the soft, shifting sounds of people settling in for a long trip. I closed my eyes.

"St. Louis! St. Louis!"

I jolted awake. Dazed and aching, I sat up and stared around me. Other passengers were stirring, too, checking their watches, digging into packs and bags. They murmured to each other about making calls from pay phones and catching cabs. The door to our car banged open, and a uniformed conductor shouted, "St. Louis! This train departs again in forty-three minutes!"

Abruptly, the rocking motion ceased. The song of the wheels gave way to the thump of doors near and distant. My mouth was parched, and I felt rumpled and dirty. I longed for something cold to drink.

While I slept, my purse had fallen to the floor. The clasp had come undone. Kleenex and lipstick were scattered under my seat. I gathered everything up and rummaged for a comb.

Hoisting my pack, I stood up on wobbly legs. I felt as though the train was still swaying along, and for a few moments I couldn't quite find my balance. Slowly, shakily, I made my way to the door and clambered down the steps to the platform.

I wondered what St. Louis looked like. In the midnight drabness of the train station, I could have been anywhere. St. Louis had the same dreary washrooms, the same sad candy and soda machines, the same haggard people I had seen in Chicago. In the washroom I pawed through my backpack and unearthed my toothbrush and toothpaste. Bending above the sink, I caught my reflection in the mirror. Bloodshot eyes stared from a thin, hollow face. Despite the comb, my hair was knotted and unkempt. I hadn't looked this bad since the last time I was in the hospital.

I sat on a plastic chair and hunted for my comb again. My purse was a mess, the comb buried under my wallet, lip gloss, and tissues.

Then it dawned on me. Somebody, some stranger with evil intentions, had rifled through my purse while I was asleep.

By some miracle my wallet was still there, and for a moment I thought it was untouched. But it was strangely flat and lifeless. The money compartment was completely empty. All those crisp new bills had vanished forever.

Desperately, without hope, I rifled through my purse. My money, my prize money from the Wisconsin Art Foundation, was gone. Stolen.

If I hadn't been so frightened, I would have been furious. But I had no energy to waste on anger. I was alone in the St. Louis train station. I had just been robbed. And somehow, I had to get to New Orleans.

I remembered what Blake said as we made our

way to Union Station. Don't panic. If you don't panic, you can figure out what to do.

My backpack had been safe under my head. The thief hadn't touched it. Thank goodness I had remembered Dad's warning about never keeping all my cash in one place. I still had a hundred dollars in one of the inside zipper compartments. And I had my round-trip train ticket. I could still get to New Orleans and back. I would manage somehow.

I went to the sink again and washed my face. If only there was somewhere I could take a shower! I could think more clearly if I felt clean! My purse dangled from my shoulder, and I kept a close watch on my backpack. From now on, I'd never let my belongings out of my sight!

The door to the washroom swished open. A large, round, middle-aged woman came in and took a place at the sink next to mine. She opened a makeup case and began to apply her lipstick and eye shadow. She looked a little bit like Aunt Kath, I thought. I wondered how Mom's day had been, with Aunt Kath at the lake. Maybe I should call home right now. Mom and Dad were probably wide-awake, miserable with worry. I didn't have to tell them where I was. I could just say I was safe. The conductor said we had forty-three minutes. That gave me plenty of time . . .

Beside me, the woman set down her makeup brush. She stared straight at me.

Why had I assumed that the thief was a he?

Women are thieves, too, I reminded myself. I didn't like the way this lady looked at me. She seemed so interested, as though she knew all about me.

I stuffed my toothbrush back into my pack. I was slipping my arms through the straps when the woman spoke up. "I know where I saw you!" she exclaimed. "You were just on the ten-o'clock news! You're the girl with that awful disease!"

11

For a moment I stared at the woman in astonishment. How did she recognize me? How did she know that I had Hodgkin's disease? I couldn't quite grasp what she had said.

"It was you!" she repeated, stepping closer. "I says to my husband, 'Frank,' I says. 'That poor girl's mother, she must be tearing her hair out by the fistful.' "

"I couldn't have been on the ten-o'clock news," I protested, backing away. "At ten o'clock I was on the train!"

"They showed your picture," the woman insisted. "I couldn't forget you — you look just like my niece, Pauline. The same nose, the same eyes — you could be sisters, the two of you. I says to my husband, 'Keep on the lookout, Frank! There's a five-thousand-dollar reward for this one.' "

The ten-o'clock news? A reward? I couldn't take it in.

"It wasn't me!" I said. "Nobody'd give five thousand dollars for me!"

I grabbed the handle and flung the door wide. "Oh, no you don't!" the woman cried, as I stepped outside. "Hold it right there!"

I never would have guessed she could move so fast! She lunged at me, reaching for me with both arms outstretched. I dodged around a row of chairs, but she was right behind me, panting and shouting, "Come here, you!"

"Norma Jean! What do you think you're doing?" A man rushed forward and seized her by the arm. He was even larger and rounder than she was. It had to be Frank.

"Stop her!" Norma Jean shrieked, squirming to get away. "She's the one we saw on TV!"

"Do you want to get us arrested again?" Frank demanded, giving her arm a shake. "Remember what happened last time? You grabbed a guy you saw on *America's Most Wanted*, and it turned out to be the mayor's favorite nephew!"

There weren't a lot of people in the train station at that time of night. But every one of them gathered to see what was going on. They closed in tightly around us. I couldn't escape.

"Look at her, Frank!" Norma Jean cried. "That face! Where have you seen that face before? Tell me the truth!"

Frank inspected me for the first time. I had no idea what Pauline looked like. I didn't know how to conceal the resemblance. Trapped, helpless, I stared back in sheer terror.

"Well, maybe," he conceded. "There *is* something about the eyes."

"Call Security!" Norma Jean shouted. "Five thousand dollars! That's our trip to Hawaii!"

Frank let go of her arm. She made another lunge for me, and again I jumped aside. But by now it was too late. The crowd parted for a uniformed officer. Norma Jean's dream of surf and sun was about to come true.

"What's going on here?" The officer who stepped up to us was a woman. She was young and petite, but to me she was scary all the same.

"We saw this little girl on Channel Seven!" Norma Jean said, her face flushed with excitement. "She ran away from home! She's supposed to be in the hospital!"

The officer looked at me doubtfully. "What's your name?" she asked. "Where are your parents?"

I was finished. They'd send me home in handcuffs. I'd never get to New Orleans, and Frank and Norma Jean would be on the next flight to Honolulu.

"Well?" the officer demanded. "What's your name? Let's start with that."

"Louisa! Louisa Grace Pritchard, where have you been?"

A tall, dark-skinned woman strode toward us.

From the first instant, she conveyed the feeling that she was in charge, and her orders would be obeyed.

"Come on this instant!" she told me. "Everybody's waiting!"

"Is she with you?" the policewoman asked her.

"She *should* be!" the woman declared. "The bus is all set to leave!"

The policewoman nodded, understanding. "You're a teacher?"

The woman handed her an ID card. "I'm Miss Rebecca Tilden, Director of the Angel Voices Gospel Choir," she announced. "We're on a nationwide tour."

The policewoman was intimidating, but Miss Rebecca Tilden was scarier by far. She glared at me. "What're you doing, Louisa, wandering off on your own? Creating a public disturbance! It's disgraceful! Let's go!"

Maybe she wanted reward money, too. She might be trying to snatch me away from Norma Jean so she could claim the five thousand dollars herself.

I opened my mouth to tell the officer who I was. But in that instant, Miss Rebecca Tilden clamped her hand onto my shoulder, and I looked into her face. Our eyes met. She gave me a sly, knowing wink.

I had no reason to trust her. She could be a kidnapper, or a serial killer. Still, when she winked at me like that, I felt that she was on my side.

"I'm sorry," I said. "I just went to the ladies' room."

"She looks exactly like that girl that — " Norma Jean began feebly.

"Does she look like she belongs in a hospital?" Frank snapped. "This one's in perfect health!"

"Oh, well," Norma Jean sighed, turning away at last. "I guess I'll have to keep looking."

The crowd disbanded. The policewoman smiled at me. "I hope that woman didn't upset you, honey," she said.

"It's okay," I told her. "She just thought I was somebody else."

Meekly I followed Miss Tilden out of the train station, onto the quiet night street. A bus waited, its engine rumbling with impatience. "Now," she said, taking my shoulders and turning me to face her again. "I know your name isn't Louisa Grace Pritchard, and I know you probably can't sing a do re mi! But it seems to me you're in trouble. You've come to the attention of a whole lot of people. If I were you, I'd get aboard this bus and put some miles between myself and them."

I nodded. You didn't argue with Miss Tilden. I climbed aboard and she pointed me to a seat. She said something to the driver, and with a grinding of gears, we were off.

The bus was filled with kids. In the dim light I saw that most of them were in their teens. For the first few miles, people kept busy passing food back and forth. I was too bewildered to pay much attention. Somehow my journey had gone totally off course. I had lost *The City of New Orleans*. And I was wanted, a missing person. There was a five-thousand-dollar price on my head.

My picture had appeared on the ten-o'clock news. Mom and Dad hadn't waited for me to turn up on my own. They must have called the police first, and then contacted a reporter. Somehow they made people listen.

If I could have reached a phone right then, I would have called them. I would have told them I was sorry a thousand times, and begged them to forgive me for causing them so much worry. But I was imprisoned on the bus. I didn't even know where I was headed. I was wandering the roadways of Missouri, on tour with the Angel Voices Gospel Choir.

I must have fallen asleep again, leaning on my lumpy backpack. Suddenly Miss Tilden loomed above me, calling, "Louisa! Rise and shine!"

I looked out my window, expecting another grim bus station. But we weren't even in a town. All I could see were trees. They seemed to stretch for miles in every direction.

"Everybody out!" Miss Tilden ordered, in her

severest tone. "Time for a little warm-up!"

"Can't we change first?" one of the girls pleaded.

"First lift your voice to the morning!" Miss Tilden replied. "Then you can think about the world."

I received no more instructions. Apparently I was supposed to follow the others. Stumbling with weariness, I descended the steps into the faint early-morning chill. For a few minutes we all followed Miss Tilden through the woods. Little by little the fresh air woke me up. I noticed the chatter of birds, and the swift shadow of a squirrel in a leap overhead. At last the trees thinned out, and we stood in a dewy meadow. Yellow daisies danced around our feet in the long grass.

Miss Tilden gestured with her hands, and we arranged ourselves in a semicircle before her. "Some loosening-up exercises," she said. "Reach for the sky!"

All around me, arms rose into the air. Like the others, I reached up and up, stretching ever higher, as though some wonderful prize hung just beyond my fingertips. Then slowly, slowly, we bent forward, down and down, until our hands brushed the earth. When we did exercises like that in gym at school, everyone groaned and complained. Somehow it was different out here, so early in the day. For a few moments I thought I knew what Miss Tilden meant when she said, "Reach for the sky."

After the exercise routine, Miss Tilden took out a pitch pipe and played a single, clear note. Suddenly the air filled with voices, climbing and sliding up and down the scale. I was never much of a singer, but I couldn't help joining in. "Mi o mi o mi," and again, a step higher, "Mi o mi o mi . . ."

" 'Shall We Gather by the River?' " Miss Tilden called. She gave the pitch once more, and the familiar old hymn swelled out over the meadow. At first I tried to sing the words I knew, but soon I fell quiet. As one song followed another, I was happy just to listen. The singers were girls and boys, black and white, and their ages seemed to range from twelve to twenty. Whatever their outward differences, they blended their voices in joyful harmony. Despite the wear of travel, they sang a celebration. It was all about being alive on a new day.

Afterward the bus took us into town. We were parceled out to people's homes in threes and fours. I went with two other girls to the Bennett family. Mrs. Bennett let us all take long, delicious showers. When we felt human again, she served up French toast with bacon, and fresh peaches from a tree in her yard. None of the girls asked where I had come from, or where I intended to go. I had the feeling that my arrival was nothing unusual. Maybe it was Miss Tilden's custom to adopt strangers in railroad stations. Everyone called me Louisa. I didn't set them straight.

As we cleared the table, Mrs. Bennett switched on the radio. Brush fires raged in California, the news announcer told us. There was another scandal in Washington. "And authorities are seeking a Wisconsin teenager who disappeared from her home sometime yesterday morning."

I froze, a bottle of syrup in my hand. But nobody else seemed to be listening. The announcer went on drily. "The girl suffers from Hodgkin's disease, and is in urgent need of medical treatment. Now for today's weather. We expect a high of eighty-seven, cooling tonight to fifty-five . . ."

It was only the roughest sketch of a story, tucked in front of the weather report. How many people heard it, and wondered who this "Wisconsin teenager" might be? No one would guess it was me. Today I was Louisa Grace Pritchard of the Angel Voices Gospel Choir.

The concert was held that afternoon at the Second Baptist Church on Main Street. I got a front-row seat, as though I were a guest of honor. I never knew that gospel music could be so exciting and so much fun. Out in the audience, we clapped along, stamped our feet, and pitched in on the refrains. But the concert itself was nothing compared with the beauty of that daybreak practice session.

Reality closed in when the concert was over. As

we piled back onto the bus, anxiety folded in on me. Part of me longed to take up Louisa's vagabond life and travel forever with my new friends. But back home in Madison, Mom and Dad were desperate. And somewhere in New Orleans, Sister Euphrasia waited with her hands of healing.

We were heading back to St. Louis now. There would be an all-night train ride, one of the girls told me. Tulsa, Oklahoma, was the choir's next stop.

We clambered aboard the bus again, and waved the town farewell. I leaned back in my seat and tried to think. In my mind I pictured a gigantic wall map. St. Louis was marked with a big red X. One arrow pointed north to Madison, Wisconsin. Another pointed south, to New Orleans.

"Are you ready to talk now?"

Miss Tilden stood in the aisle. I wasn't afraid of her anymore. I patted the empty seat beside me, and she sat down.

"You probably think I'm a runaway or something," I began. "But it isn't like that. I'm going home as soon as I can."

"Well then," she said, "what's your trouble?"

I wanted to tell her my whole story. But I didn't quite dare. She had protected me from Norma Jean and the policewoman. But she was still a grown-up, after all. She belonged to that world of reason and responsibility that all adults seemed to inhabit. If she knew the truth about me, the case would be closed. She'd call my parents and ship me home. I'd have no choice left.

"I started out searching for someone," I said cautiously. "It's important. It's — it might save my life."

"You'd better go find that person then, don't you think?"

I nodded. "But my parents are worried about me," I said. "They went on the news and everything. They're offering a reward."

"Can't you call and tell them you're all right?" she asked.

"They'll try to talk me into going home," I explained. "If I heard their voices, I think I would. I'd just give up."

"Then you need to get them a message somehow," Miss Tilden said. "Let them know you're safe, without talking to them directly."

"Yes," I said slowly. "I'll think about that. Maybe I can."

All the way back to St. Louis, I turned her words over in my head. By the time the bus reached the train station, a simple plan had come to me. I knew what I was going to do.

12

I said good-bye to my new friends one by one as we got off the bus in St. Louis. "You're ready to go on your way," Miss Tilden said with one of her rare, shining smiles. "Those bounty hunters have all packed up and gone by now."

"There might be new ones, though," I said. "I'll have to be careful."

"Tell me the truth," she said. "Is there anything we can do to help?"

I thought of the money in my wallet, those two fifty-dollar bills between me and destitution. I had my train ticket, and I could stretch my money to cover a few snacks and cheap meals. But who knew what lurked ahead? I steered away from the thought. It was too frightening.

I was brought up never to ask for money from anyone. And even now, when I was breaking all kinds of rules, I couldn't break that one.

"I'm okay," I assured her. "I just have to catch my train."

"Well, I wish you the best of everything," she said. "You're going to do fine."

When she hugged me good-bye, I was afraid I'd start to cry. I stepped back, struggling for control, and took her outstretched hand. "Thank you," I said fervently. "You really saved me! It's been a wonderful day!"

"I hope to see you again sometime," Miss Tilden said. "Practice your scales. One of these days we'll get you to sing."

She gave my hand a parting squeeze, and pressed a folded paper against my palm. "Here's a note for you," she said, turning away quickly. "Don't read it till you're on the train."

Even when she was out of sight, Miss Rebecca Tilden commanded obedience. I slipped the note into my purse. I wouldn't dream of opening it until I was safely aboard *The City of New Orleans*.

It was a few minutes past midnight. My train would leave in forty minutes. I had plenty of time to make a phone call.

I found a row of pay phones and counted out all of the change I had. A dollar and eighty-seven cents — that ought to be enough. I punched the number of Dad's office, and started feeding in quarters and dimes. My heart raced as I heard the faraway ringing of the phone on Dad's desk. At this time of night, I knew he wouldn't be there to answer it.

There was a faint click on the third ring. Then,

113

clear and unmistakable, Dad spoke in my ear. "You have reached the voice mail of Eric Thomas. Please leave a message after the tone, or press zero to reach an operator . . ."

His calm, familiar voice filled me with longing. For a moment I couldn't say anything.

"Deposit thirty-five cents for the next two minutes," said a stern mechanical voice. I dropped the coins into the slot. "Dad," I tried again. "It's me, Shannon. I just want to let you know I'm okay. I mean, I'm not kidnapped or anything like that." I stopped. Somewhere behind me an announcer called, "Amtrak for Pittsburgh and Philadelphia, boarding at Gate Twenty-four . . ."

What else could I say? I didn't dare explain where I was — they'd put the FBI on my trail. And I certainly couldn't tell them where I was heading. "I'll be home as soon as I can," I promised. "It's just that there's something I've got to do first. But I'm all right. Don't worry about me." I paused for another moment, but I couldn't think of anything to add. "Well," I said. "I love you. I'll see you pretty soon. Bye."

I wondered how long it would be before Dad got my message. If he was busy with cops and reporters, he wouldn't go to the office. But he might be waiting for a ransom call, orders on where to leave a bag of unmarked bills. The police had probably issued precise instructions about what he should say and do. Yes, I decided, Dad would check his voice mail faithfully.

There must be plenty of excitement back home right now! Police officers staking out the house, reporters standing in line for interviews, neighbors peering from their windows and whispering rumors back and forth. It wasn't fair that I had to miss it all. For a wild moment I longed to be there, enjoying the adventure. Well, if I was there, none of that would be happening, I reminded myself.

I was getting pretty good at following signs and arrows. Without much trouble I found my gate. I joined a dozen or so other waiting passengers on the plastic chairs. No one even glanced in my direction. I allowed myself to feel almost safe.

Three chairs down, someone had abandoned a copy of the *St. Louis Post-Dispatch*. I slid over and picked it up. Spreading it open before me I felt safe, shielded from the public view. I scanned a couple of stories about warfare — Africa, Bosnia, the Middle East. On the national scene there were those California brush fires again, and the federal deficit. And at the bottom of page 1 a headline read, "SEARCH WIDENS FOR TEEN WITH CANCER, MISSING SINCE THURSDAY." My picture smiled out from the page.

"Madison, Wisconsin," the story ran. "Shannon Thomas, age thirteen, was reported missing from her home at five forty-five P.M. Thursday, July 26." At five forty-five? How could that be? Mom and Dad should both have been out until six.

"The teen has been undergoing treatment for a rare form of cancer for the past three years," the article went on. " 'She was scheduled to go back to the hospital for more chemotherapy next week,' explained Peggy Thomas, forty-four, the girl's mother. 'We think she couldn't face it again.'

"Shannon recently received a thousand-dollar prize in a statewide drawing contest. Police theorize that she is living on the prize money. A reward of five thousand dollars is offered for information leading to the girl's safe return. 'We don't have any idea where she headed,' Ms. Thomas explained. 'We're alerting media all over the country. We just want to know that she's safe. We want her back with us.' "

My eyes burned with tears. I tried to brush them away, but they kept falling. I held the newspaper closer to my face, and hoped no one could tell that I was crying.

"*The City of New Orleans* is now boarding!" called an overhead speaker. "All ticket-holding passengers should board at Gate Nineteen."

I tore out the article and slipped it into my pocketbook. I didn't want to leave it there on the seat, where somebody else could read it. But the *St. Louis Post Dispatch* must print thousands of copies, I reminded myself. They lay on living-room sofas and kitchen tables and park benches all over the city. And this was only one paper among hundreds.

Dizzily, I got up and followed the other passengers to the train. An elderly woman turned to look at me. She wore a rumpled pink sweater, too much lipstick, and a curious stare. My stomach lurched with fear. Had she recognized me? Or was she merely surprised to see someone my age traveling alone? I hastened down the platform and took a seat in a different car. No one followed me. Nobody called my name.

When the train started moving at last, I unfolded the article and read it again. It was just like the story about the drawing contest — full of mistakes. They called my everyday, garden-variety Hodgkin's disease "a rare form of cancer." They doubled my art contest winnings. And they still couldn't get my age right. This time they made me too young, thirteen instead of fourteen.

They could have reprinted the photo that appeared when I won the art contest. But for some reason they used my yearbook picture instead. It was taken last October. I had just finished a round of chemotherapy, and I wore a wig because I was bald as a hard-boiled egg. The wig looked nothing like my own hair. It was too dark, too thick and straight. At the time I had been horrified. I cried the first day I wore it to school; everyone would know it wasn't real. But today, looking at that old photo, I rejoiced. With my own light-brown curls, I had a perfect disguise.

The train clattered along the track, carrying me farther and farther south. I thought of the map in the atlas at home. I was well out of Illinois now, somewhere deep into Missouri. We'd cross Arkansas during the night, and in the morning we'd enter Louisiana.

Reading that newspaper article had really shaken me. I still felt a bit light-headed from the shock. This vague dizzy feeling might be exhaustion, too, I reminded myself. I tried to count my hours of sleep since I left Madison, but I was too tired to add them up. There weren't many, I knew that much.

The car was air-conditioned. It may have been a hot summer night outside, but the inside temperature dropped lower and lower. I dug my sweater out of my backpack, but it hardly made a difference. I curled into a ball on the narrow seat, trying to wrap my legs with my arms. I couldn't get warm.

Through the long night, I tumbled in and out of a ragged sleep. At last I came fully awake as the first morning light filtered through the windows. The train stood still. In the aisle, people maneuvered bags from the overhead racks and edged toward the door. "Little Rock!" the conductor shouted. "Little Rock, Arkansas!"

I sat up, shivering. With trembling hands I pawed through my backpack again, searching vainly for something warm to put on. I found nothing but flimsy shorts and tank tops. I should have packed long johns and mittens instead!

When I stood up, the floor seemed to ripple beneath my feet. I grabbed a metal pole for support, and swayed toward the door. Gratefully I stepped down into the steamy summer morning. I stood still, waiting for my hands and feet to thaw. Slowly, inch by inch, I warmed up.

I found a snack counter and bought some orange juice and a couple of doughnuts to go. In the washroom I brushed my teeth and splashed water on my face. Everywhere I went, I kept a lookout for anyone who might be studying me too carefully. Bounty hunters, that's what Miss Rebecca Tilden called them.

Suddenly I remembered the note Miss Tilden had given me as we said good-bye. I opened it when I got back to my seat on the train. As I read, I could hear her voice behind the clear, simple words. "It doesn't matter that I don't know your real name," she had written. "I know you're headed somewhere important. When you get there, you'll find out what you have to do. Just remember, there's somebody watching over you."

The note was signed, "With love, Miss Rebecca Tilden and the Angel Voices Gospel Choir."

There was another folded page within the envelope. On the outside, Miss Tilden wrote, "Here's something to help you on your travels." Inside were five twenty-dollar bills.

I slipped everything back into the envelope and held it for a long time. I could never thank her enough. Even if she were standing here in front of me and I talked and talked, I couldn't thank her enough.

The air-conditioning was still turned on high, but I wasn't cold anymore. In fact, I felt quite warm now, as though I had carried the heat of Little Rock onto the train with me. I stuffed my sweater into my pack and sipped at my orange juice. I knew I should be hungry, but my doughnut tasted like cardboard. The thought of food, any food, was repulsive.

This was weariness, I told myself. I was tired and stressed out. For two days now I'd been running. I couldn't expect to feel my best.

Somewhere behind my eyes, a pinprick of pain blazed to life. It swelled larger, pounding in time to the swaying of the train. My throat felt parched. I took another swallow of juice. It didn't help.

I pressed my hand to my forehead, but the pain grew larger. I cupped my face between my hands and closed my eyes. My hands traced down my burning cheeks and along my neck. Suddenly my fingers paused, sensing what was there even before the truth registered in my brain. It was nothing, I told myself. Just my imagination. But my fingers couldn't lie. Small and hard, like a lima bean nestled beneath my skin, I felt a lump.

13

Two rows in front of me, an old man complained to his wife all day. He said the food in the dining car wasn't fit for a cocker spaniel. The conductors had the manners of New York cabbies. Railroad service would never be what it was in the 1940s.

When they announced that we would pull into New Orleans more than an hour behind schedule, he exclaimed, "Didn't I tell you! They can't even read a timetable nowadays! Punctuality means nothing anymore!"

If he hadn't made such a fuss, I never would have noticed we were late. My body was burning hot, yet I shivered with chills. Again and again my fingers sought that ominous lump on the left side of my neck. It was always there. The bounty hunters might fail to track me down. But my fate had caught up with me all the same.

Dr. O'Brien had warned that this could happen. Any weakness, exhaustion, or high fever could mean that my remission was over. Any mysterious lump could be another enlarged lymph node, the most treacherous sign of all.

If I ever had symptoms like these, Dr. O'Brien had said, I must call right away. But who could I call now? I was hundreds of miles from home, beyond the reach of anyone I knew. There was no one to help me.

The door to our car banged open. "New Orleans!" the conductor's voice boomed.

All around me people were coming to life. They stretched and yawned, laughed and muttered, and searched for their scattered belongings. I went through the motions of checking my purse and backpack. I was conscious enough to make sure Miss Tilden's money was safely stowed in my pack, while the rest of my cash was in my wallet. I'd always remember Dad's advice now. *Never keep all your money in one place.*

I stood up shakily and hung onto the back of the seat, letting the other passengers file out ahead of me. I was the last person to leave the car. At the top of the steps I hesitated. The train was my final refuge. As long as I was on board, I didn't have to make any decisions. From now on, I was adrift. A decision had to be made, and I couldn't think clearly. I had no idea what to do.

"Come on, Miss," the conductor said, smiling up at me from the platform. He held out his hand to help me down.

There were three long steps. I put out my foot and lowered myself carefully. One step . . . two . . .

My knees buckled. Suddenly I pitched forward, aiming headlong for the pavement. The conductor flung out his arms and caught me in midair. He set me down gently, and held my arm as if he was afraid I would fall again.

"Are you all right?" he asked.

"I'm fine," I said. A handful of people stopped to stare at me. Had any of them read the paper? Turned on the radio? Watched the news?

"Maybe you should sit down," the conductor said. I didn't argue. He led me to a chair in the waiting room. I sat down, feeling foolish and grateful both at once.

"Have you got any luggage?" the conductor asked. "I'll get it for you."

I shook my head, and touched the pack strapped to my back. "No, really. I've just got this."

The conductor looked down at me with a worried frown. He was heavyset, with streaks of gray in his thinning hair. "Is someone meeting you?" he asked.

It was time to trot out my Aunt Mary again. I was almost starting to believe in her myself. But when I opened my mouth, I heard myself say, "No. I'm here alone."

Another chill seized me. I wrapped my arms around myself, trying to get my shivering under control.

For a moment the conductor watched me uncertainly. Then he reached out and touched my forehead, the way Dad or Mom might have done if I were safe at home. "You've got a high temperature!" he said. "You need to see a doctor."

"No!" I cried in panic. Doctors didn't have the answers I wanted. They would slap me into a hospital, strap me down, and stick me with a dozen needles. I felt sick now, but I'd be a lot sicker when they got through with me. No, I thought. I'd come to New Orleans to get away from doctors.

Contact us right away, Dr. O'Brien had said. *Don't lose valuable time . . .*

The conductor was still watching me. I couldn't sit here forever. I had to do something.

I brought the words out slowly, with an enormous effort. "Well," I said, "maybe I should see somebody after all."

After that, things happened very quickly. The conductor led me to an office at the rear of the station. The sign on the door read, TRAVELERS AID SOCIETY. He handed me over to a brisk young woman named Miss Fontaine, who explained that she was a social worker.

So far, all I'd seen of New Orleans was the inside of the railway station. But Miss Fontaine's drawl reminded me that I was now in the South. When she asked for my name, I told her I was Louisa Grace Pritchard.

"Yes. All right." She wrote something onto a

blue form. By the cool tone in her voice, I knew she didn't believe me. "And where are you going, Louisa?"

"I'm on my way to my Aunt Mary's," I said. To head off her next question I added, "I haven't got her phone number. I mean — there isn't a phone. She's out on the boat."

"I see," Miss Fontaine said, with a deepening frown. "And just how are you supposed to get in touch with her then?"

My head pounded. Why hadn't I planned a better story? I couldn't think fast enough to invent one now.

"Tell me the truth," Miss Fontaine said, looking me in the eye. "Did you run away from home?"

I couldn't lie my way out of this one. Miss Fontaine might not have read the paper, but she had her suspicions about me. If she kept me in her office much longer, I would blurt out the whole story.

There was only one escape. "I'm sick," I said. "I think I need to go to the hospital."

I didn't have to do any acting. Miss Fontaine gave me a long, hard look, and pulled a thermometer out of her desk drawer. It was one of those little strips that you press to your forehead. She watched the numbers change color and murmured, "One-oh-two."

There were more questions then. She wanted to know about Aunt Mary, about anyone she could call who would take charge of me. I offered no names, no numbers. At last she picked up the phone. "Yes," she said. "This is Travelers Aid at the train station. We need an ambulance."

The paramedics were a man and a woman. Both of them were young, like a couple of college kids. There was a sort of bed in the back of the ambulance, and they told me to lie down. I hadn't had a chance to lie full-length since I left Madison two days ago. I stretched out my legs and closed my eyes. The female paramedic tucked a blanket around me. Almost at once I began to feel better. I knew I should use the time to get my story in order. At the hospital I would face plenty of questions from doctors, nurses, and social workers. But thinking took energy. I only wanted to lie motionless, lulled by the steady hum of the motor.

I'd been in and out of hospitals more times than I could count. But strangely, I had never arrived in an ambulance before. They delivered me straight to the emergency room, where a new team of paramedics took over. They peered and probed, taking my "vital signs" — heart rate, temperature, blood pressure. "What's your name?" a male voice asked beside my head. I pretended I didn't hear him. I didn't even open my eyes.

Gentle hands lifted me, set me down again. I must be on a stretcher, rolling along a hospital corridor. I kept my eyes closed. I felt safer some-how, not looking at the people around me.

The stretcher came to a stop, and everyone went away. I don't know how long I was parked there. Footsteps hurried back and forth, loud-speakers shouted messages, and somewhere a baby cried. I pushed it all away from me, and drifted to sleep.

I woke to a beam of light shining into my face. My eyes popped open. A tall, skinny nurse bent above me, smiling encouragement. "Louisa," she drawled, "can you hear me?"

I wasn't fully awake, but I managed to nod. The nurse smiled more broadly. I read the name on her badge: Patti Lou Morgan. "You're conscious," she said. "Can you answer a few questions for me?"

I had eluded Miss Fontaine, but that was just a delaying tactic. I was really caught this time. There was nowhere left to run.

"I know you can talk," said Patti Lou, when I didn't open my mouth. "You talked in the ambu-lance."

That was true. I thanked the paramedics. I told them how nice it felt to lie down instead of scrunching up on the seat in a train. They didn't ask me any questions.

Don't waste valuable time . . . I had to speak up. I had to explain that I had Hodgkin's disease, and show her the lump in my neck. She was a nurse. Maybe she could help me.

If I told her about my illness, I'd have to explain what I was doing in New Orleans. I'd have to tell her about running away to find Sister Euphrasia. They'd call Mom and Dad and put me on the next flight back to Madison.

If I gave up now, if I returned home without completing my mission, all of that effort and worry would be in vain. But if I found Sister Euphrasia, if she could really help me, then every tortured moment would prove worthwhile in the end.

"How do you feel?" Patti Lou persisted. "You need to tell us."

Actually, I felt a bit better. I was still a little feverish, but the chills no longer rattled me to pieces. I wanted to say that I was fine now, that my little rest had done wonders. But she wouldn't believe me. I lay still and said nothing.

"We can't help you, Louisa, if you don't tell us what's wrong." I heard a note of irritation in her voice. Patti Lou Morgan was near the end of her patience.

Escape was still possible after all. I closed my eyes and didn't speak.

I had discovered the perfect strategy. I was like one of those witnesses in a courtroom drama, invoking the Fifth Amendment. *I refuse to answer on the grounds that it may incriminate me.* I had a constitutional right to remain silent.

Patti Lou fired one question after another. She

seemed to think that sooner or later she'd hit the right one, and a fountain of answers would burst forth from me. How old was I? Where was I from? Where was my family? Did anyone know I was here? I had nothing to say, no matter what she asked.

Finally she gave up. She shrugged her shoulders, said a brusque good-bye, and left me in peace. I lay in a narrow cubicle with partitions on either side of my stretcher. A white curtain hung across the door. Somewhere close by, someone snored noisily. Whoever it was had the right idea. This was my opportunity to sleep. I must gather my strength. When the time came, I would know what to do.

I don't know how long I slept. When I woke at last, I was very thirsty. My fever had almost disappeared. I slid hopeful fingers along my neck, but the lump had not been as cooperative. It was definitely still there. Had it grown a little bigger?

Somewhere beyond my cubicle, dishes clattered. The curtain slid aside to reveal Patti Lou Morgan, wheeling a tray table with a glass of juice and a covered dish. An older nurse was with her this time. She was called Nancy Moreau, according to her nametag.

"You hungry?" Patti Lou asked. She pushed the tray ahead of her through the door.

I sat up, nodding, and reached for the glass of

juice. If the nurses had been meaner, or more clever, they might have held it back as a bribe, to try to make me talk. Instead they let me empty the glass before they started in with their questions again.

This time they began from a different angle. Why didn't I talk? they wanted to know. I could trust them. There was nothing to be afraid of. No one here would hurt me. They wanted to help.

I shook my head and opened the covered dish. They had brought me supper — chicken and rice covered with some kind of reddish sauce. Hospital food was usually horrible, but I was so hungry that I dug right in. To my amazement, the chicken was delicious. I remembered what Blake had said about eating in New Orleans. If the hospital fare was this good, I'd love to sample the restaurants.

Patti Lou and Nancy stood in the doorway, watching with satisfaction. I took a breath to tell them how good everything tasted. But I stopped myself just in time. If I spoke at all, everything would unravel. I carried so much in my mind, I wouldn't be able to keep it from spilling out.

The food wasn't the only unique thing about this New Orleans hospital. The nurses seemed to have all the time in the world. Back in Madison, the staff rushed from one room to the next, answering call buttons, checking IVs, giving medications. When they weren't tending to patients, the nurses were busy writing in medical charts. But Patti Lou and Nancy hovered over me, filling my cubicle with their cheerful chatter. I felt as though I were the only person under their care.

I wasn't alone here, I reminded myself. I was in a crowded hospital in the middle of a big city. For some reason I had been singled out for special attention. Maybe I was a novelty. I was the kid with the weird name and no known relations, the kid who refused to utter a word. I presented a challenge to them. They were determined to make a breakthrough.

"Okay, we get the picture," Nancy said as I scraped up the last of the sauce. "You're not going to tell us who you are. Maybe we can tell *you* a few things instead."

I turned to study her, suddenly on the alert. She smiled an encouraging, trust-me smile. "You came in on the train from St. Louis. That's pretty far away. There may be people who are concerned about you, have you thought about that?"

I nodded. I could answer with gestures; it didn't quite feel like cheating. Still, I had to be careful. She could lead me into a trap.

"The doctor will be here to examine you pretty soon," Patti Lou put in. "You've got to tell him what's the matter."

Nancy glanced at her, frowning. Apparently she wanted to handle me herself. "It's very important," she said, coming down hard on the words.

"If you have any serious medical condition, you must tell us what it is. It could be a matter of life and death."

She stepped back a pace, as though to make room for her final words. They billowed out to hang in the air like great, colored balloons. "You must tell the truth!"

Yes, I thought, I was more than a novelty and a challenge. My hair was lighter, I'd put on a few pounds, but they suspected who I was. I was the kid they'd seen on the news. And if they turned me in, they earned a five-thousand-dollar reward.

14

The three of us were playing a game. Nancy and Patti Lou knew, but they pretended not to know. I pretended not to know that I knew that they knew. It was so complicated I almost laughed out loud. But if I laughed, they would know that I knew that they knew . . .

So I silently pleaded the Fifth Amendment, and waited. As long as they didn't make me put on a hospital gown, as long as they didn't hook me up to an IV, I could still get away.

At last Patti Lou wheeled my tray away, and Nancy said breezily, "We'll let you rest a few minutes. The doctor will be here in a little while." I nodded my understanding, and lifted my hand in farewell.

They had left me alone. I waited through a long minute, giving them time to go away. Then I slid off the stretcher and picked up my purse and my backpack. I peered around the edge of my curtain into a long, narrow hallway. It was littered with empty wheelchairs, gurneys, and boxes, but I didn't see any nurses. Down at one end, two old women in bathrobes stood talking. A man with an aluminum walker made his careful way toward me. Nobody cheered him on. No one seemed to be watching at all.

I hestitated, clutching the doorframe. But something urged me forward, as though I had no choice. This was my chance. I couldn't throw it away.

I stepped into the hall, letting the curtain fall into place behind me. Feeling hopelessly conspicuous, I passed a row of curtained cubicles like my own. As though I were channel-surfing, I caught a patchwork of conversations along the way. " . . . ever since Monday, I can't put weight on it . . ." " . . . call my wife, she doesn't know . . ." " . . . how much longer do I have to . . ."

I rounded the corner into a wider, busier corridor. Here I could blend in with the visitors, all those other fortunate souls dressed in street clothes. I was so used to hospitals that the maze of halls didn't scare me. Within a few minutes I found the main lobby. It was just as I expected — the usual gift shop, information desk, and stiff vinyl-covered couches. Hospital lobbies were alike the world over, I decided, just like train stations. I didn't know where I'd go once I got outside, but I headed for the revolving door.

"Louisa! Louisa Pritchard, where do you think you're going?"

I had only been Louisa Pritchard for two days. I didn't respond to the name instinctively. For a second or two I walked on, as though the voice at my back had nothing to do with me.

"Didn't you hear me? The doctor's looking for you!"

In slow motion I turned around. Patti Lou Morgan scrambled toward me, looking like a heron on her long, spindly legs. She was still playing the game. She was still pretending that she didn't know.

Without a word, I sprinted for the door and swept through to the street. I barely noticed the burst of sticky New Orleans heat. Somehow I called on every molecule of strength I possessed. I broke into a run. The heat, my fever, the lump in my neck, nothing could stop me.

The game was over. "Shannon Thomas! Stop right there!" Patti Lou shouted. I dodged into a parking lot, zigzagging among the parked cars. I leaped a guardrail and dashed across an empty lot. "Shannon!" she called again, but she was dropping behind me. Not even those heron legs could keep up with me now.

I darted down an alleyway lined with garbage pails. It led me to the rear door of a supermarket, where a man in overalls was unloading crates from a flatbed truck. The door stood open, and I flashed through. A sign scolded, EMPLOYEES ONLY, but I slipped unseen among tiers of boxes. This would be a good place to hide for a while. Patti Lou would never find me here. But some stockboy was sure to spot me, and I'd be cornered. I needed to cover distance, to put as many blocks as I could between myself and the hospital.

Slowing to a trot, I left the safety of the storeroom. The place was just like any supermarket I'd ever visited in Madison. The same music billowed from overhead, the same signs promised 39 cents off on disposable diapers. I wondered why people bothered to travel. Everywhere I went was exactly like everywhere else.

I cruised down the canned goods aisle, passed the dry breakfast cereals and shelves of bleach and laundry detergent. As I reached the automatic doors, I came to a halt. Beside the checkout counter I saw a stack of folded newspapers. My eyes were snared by the front-page headline: "MISSING GIRL SENDS MESSAGE TO DESPERATE PARENTS."

The world around me faded. I stood transfixed as I read on: "MADISON WI — A nationwide search continues for fourteen-year-old Shannon Thomas, missing since Thursday morning. The girl, who has Hodgkin's disease, is in urgent need of treatment. Shannon's parents received a message from her yesterday on a telephone answering machine. In the message, Shannon claimed that she plans to return home. 'I just want to let you know I'm not kidnapped,' the girl explained in her brief communication. 'I'll be home as soon as I can. There's something I've got to do first. But I'm all right. Don't worry about me. I love you. I'll see you pretty soon.'

"A tip from a friend leads police to suspect that Thomas may try to reach New Orleans . . ."

A tip from a friend? What friend? I'd never breathed a word to Abby, or to anyone else. No one on earth could even guess where I had gone — except Kim Smith.

A wave of dizziness swept over me again. I clutched the edge of the counter, afraid I was going to faint. I hadn't recovered after all, I thought, through the roaring in my ears. There really was something wrong with me. I couldn't go any farther. I had to go back . . . go home . . .

"Well, don't just stand there staring!" It was a woman's voice, shrill with impatience. I was blocking the aisle. The woman edged forward, glaring at me, and shouldered me out of her way.

"Hey!" I said, straightening up. She had gone without a backward glance. What did I expect? I asked myself. People were always pushing me aside.

No, that wasn't true! I had packed my bag,

boarded a bus and two trains, escaped from bounty hunters, sung with a gospel choir, and eluded a galloping nurse. I had nearly reached my final destination. I wasn't the old Shannon Thomas anymore. I had done something extraordinary, something I could never have imagined possible.

I felt my strength seeping back. It spread like sunlight through my head and body, fanning out to my arms and legs, all the way to the tips of my fingers. I let go of the counter and marched to the door. I was in New Orleans, and I was free. Before somebody found me, I had to find Sister Euphrasia.

I knew I would attract attention if I tried to run on the wide, busy sidewalk. I forced myself to walk slowly, sedately, as though I had lived here all my life and knew precisely where I was going. All I really knew was that I had to get away from the hospital. And somehow I had to find the French Quarter.

By now it was growing dark. Back in Madison, Mom and Dad insisted it wasn't safe to be out alone at night. Yet here I was, alone after sundown on the streets of a city I did not know. I might be in real danger. I needed something to eat and a place to sleep — food and shelter, the most basic necessities of life.

I walked. I walked aimlessly along dimly lit streets, searching. Office buildings towered around me like cliffs of concrete, glass, and steel. Once I wandered into a section of small wooden houses. They pressed close together, fringed by dry, ragged lawns. Lights flickered behind drawn curtains. Here and there I heard voices through an open window, or the chatter of a television. Inside those houses, people went about their evening routines — washing dishes, reading bedtime stories, watching their favorite shows. I envied them. They had no idea how fortunate they were!

I felt safe from capture by now, but the heat was a force to reckon with. Like a dense, clammy mist, it pressed upon me from all sides. I began to feel dizzy again. I longed for a tall glass of water, a cool place to sit down. But I plodded on, block after block.

The streets narrowed, and suddenly there were more people on the sidewalks. They laughed and jostled, filling the air with noise and life. They acted as if it weren't late at all, as though the important part of the day had just begun.

The houses here had an exotic look. Iron balconies leaned above the pavement, adorned with lacy ironwork designs. Some houses had heavy wrought-iron gates as well. I approached one gate and peered through. Beyond it lay a garden, moonlit and fragrant. A fountain taunted me with its cool splashing. I wished I could throw myself into the water, then sprawl on the grass to dry.

But the gate wore a heavy square padlock.

At that point, my legs rebelled. They refused to carry me another step. I sank to the ground and huddled against a wall. I couldn't just walk forever. If I was going to find Sister Euphrasia, I had to start asking questions.

Somewhere I heard a band begin to play. According to my watch, it was nine-fourteen, hardly time for a parade. But I distinctly heard trumpets, clarinets, and the pounding of drums. Curiosity pulled me to my feet once more. I followed the music to the end of the block and around the corner.

The band was playing at one end of a large city park. People crowded around to listen, applauding at the close of each number. As I drew near, the band broke into "When the Saints Come Marching In!"

"Yeah, yeah," muttered a girl in front of me. "Can't they play anything cool?"

"Hey Zil, where's Tomato?" demanded the girl next to her. "He said he'd be here."

They both turned to scan the crowd. I stepped back in amazement. They were covered with tattoos.

"You seen a punk with a Mohawk?" the girl called Zil asked me. "Wears five earrings?"

A rose blossomed from her right shoulder. Some sort of jungle vine curled down her arm. A green rhinestone glittered in her nose.

"No," I stammered. "I don't know him."

"He hangs out by the bridge," the second girl said, to prod my memory. "Came in from Brooklyn." Each of her arms was adorned with a coiled snake that twisted toward her collarbone.

"She don't know him," said Zil. "She don't know nobody around here."

They certainly didn't sound friendly. They didn't *look* friendly, either. If I had been anywhere else, I would have watched them in fascination, keeping a safe distance. But they were the first people who had spoken to me since I left the hospital. I couldn't let them slip away without asking them a few questions.

"Listen," I said. "Do you guys happen to know where the French Quarter is?"

The girl with the snakes shook her head sadly. "French Quarter, French Quarter," she repeated. "Parlay voo . . ."

"Ah, wee wee, Madame!" cried Zil. Suddenly they both doubled up with howls of laughter. They shook from side to side, moaning and hugging themselves with glee.

I tried to edge away from them, but the crowd pressed in behind me. For the moment I couldn't move. "The French Quarter!" Zil gasped. "Open your eyes, girl! Look around!"

"What planet did you fall off of?" Snakes demanded. "The French Quarter! You're in the middle of the French Quarter right now!"

15

The moment she spoke, everything fell into place. My mind flashed back to Blake, saying good-bye at Union Station in Chicago. The French Quarter was very famous, he said. It had lots of old buildings with wrought-iron decorations . . .

"Oh, sure," I said. "I was just checking. Thanks."

More than ever I wanted to get away from them. I tried to wriggle past a bulky man in a business suit, but Zil grabbed my arm. "You don't need to go anywhere," she pointed out. "You're here already." Her eyes smiled. She wasn't unfriendly after all.

"Listen," I said. "There's this person I'm trying to find. Maybe you've heard of her. She's called Sister Euphrasia."

"Sister You-What?" Snakes exclaimed. "You-Fraidy? That's a good one!"

The music rose to a crescendo. "Euphrasia!" I shouted through the din. "Sister Euphrasia!"

They shook their heads. For a few moments the music was so loud we didn't try to speak. When the song was over at last, Zil said, "This Sister Whatever, who does she hang out with?"

"I don't know," I said. "She's kind of a healer, that's all I know for sure."

Zil turned serious. "You sick or something?" she asked.

I shook my head.

At the other end of the park, someone played a saxophone. The notes spiraled up and down, weaving smooth, soft braids across the summer air. "Where'd you blow in from, anyway?" Zil asked me.

"Wisconsin," I said. Even now, lying didn't come automatically. Sometimes the truth slipped out by mistake.

"Wisconsin!" she cried, breaking into a grin. "You're the first Wisconsin I've had!"

I didn't want to ask another stupid question. I kept my mouth shut and hoped things would start to make sense.

"There was a Utah the other day," she said. "A real cool dude. Like, I bet he was a cowboy."

Snakes tried to enlighten me. "Godzilla has this thing about states," she said. "Every time she meets a new one, she thinks it's good luck."

"Is that really your name?" I asked. "Godzilla?"

"You don't like it?" she demanded. For a second

144

I thought she was angry, but then I caught the hint of a grin.

"Well," I said, "it's a little unusual."

"I know. That's why I picked it."

"They used to call me Stephanie, but now I'm Thunder," said the one with the snakes.

"We'll call you Wisconsin for now," said Zil. "Unless it brings back bad memories."

"Why would it?" I asked, puzzled.

"Wisconsin must be worse than here," she said logically. "It's the place you're running away from, right?"

I told her Wisconsin was as good a name as any. The band finished playing, and the crowd began to disperse. Thunder pointed to my backpack. "You got any eats?" she asked.

I dug out a bag of corn chips. By now they were mostly crumbs, but we passed them back and forth, crunching hungrily. "We've got to find Tomato," Thunder said. "He'll have some food."

"Come on," Zil said. "I bet I know where he is."

I trailed after them through the park. In the center stood the statue of a man on a galloping horse. "That's General Andrew Jackson," Zil told me. "He's like the guardian angel of this place. That's why they call it Jackson Square."

A boy had climbed onto the statue's pedestal, and was trying to shinny up one of the horse's legs. Not only did he wear his hair in a Mohawk;

it was dyed bright orange. I couldn't count the earrings that dangled from his left ear. Thunder and Zil raced toward him. "Tomato!" they called. "We're starving!"

Tomato jumped down. He was barefoot, and his baggy jeans were dirty and torn. "Yeah, okay," he said. "We'll scare up something. Let's go."

"Pierre's?" Zil said with a little skip.

"Sure," said Tomato. "Whatever."

They didn't bother to introduce me. Nobody seemed to care who I was or what I was doing here. Together the four of us left Jackson Square. We passed a spired cathedral like something from a medieval painting. A horse-drawn carriage clattered by. Somewhere someone played a polka on an accordion. A little farther away, a rock band broke into one of Green Day's hits. For a few minutes, we paused to watch a group of boys breakdancing on the sidewalk.

I had to amend my thinking about American cities. They weren't all the same. Never in my life had I seen anything like New Orleans.

Even from the outside, I could tell that Pierre's Restaurant was elegant. Clean, well-dressed men and women glided in and out of the canopied entrance. I pictured us marching inside with Tomato in the lead, taking possession like a ragged guerrilla army. I imagined the patrons shrieking, the maître d' wielding a broom.

But Tomato didn't try to storm the front entrance. Instead he led us through an alley to a row of trash barrels by the back door. Half a dozen other kids were there already. Zil flipped open the lid of one pail and reached in. "Chicken cordon bleu!" she cried, holding up a drumstick. *"Merci beaucoup!"*

My stomach lurched. I sat down heavily and tried not to watch as Thunder and Tomato joined in the feast. They squatted on the ground, devouring chunks of cheese, slices of French bread, carrot sticks, mushrooms, and bits of roast beef. Zil found half of a cheesecake and passed it around triumphantly.

Get her to take you to one of those fancy restaurants, Blake had told me back in Chicago. Well, here I was at Pierre's, one of the classiest places in town.

"Aren't you hungry?" asked Zil with concern.

"I ate before," I told her.

"Oh, yeah?" Tomato asked with interest. "Where'd you go?"

"I was at the hospital."

"The hospital!" Tomato cried. "The hospital's the pits! Pierre's has the best garbage in the whole city!"

We slept that night in Jackson Square. There must have been a dozen of us, girls and boys from twelve to eighteen, all huddled under the trees. No one complained. They had fled lives that were even worse than this, and they held on in spite of everything.

I searched out a spot free from broken glass, and curled up on the grass. My backpack served as a pillow. I wrapped the strap of my purse around my arm so nobody could snatch it.

Zil offered me a blanket. It was so tattered and filthy I told her I was warm enough already. I hoped I hadn't hurt her feelings. She was doing her best to make me feel welcome. Without any questions, she accepted me as a newcomer, another kid fresh off the bus.

But I would never be one of them. I belonged to a family. As soon as I found Sister Euphrasia, I was going home.

I woke at dawn to the pealing of church bells. Today was Sunday, I marveled. I had been traveling for three days. It felt like half a lifetime.

Slowly I sat up and tried to work the aches out of my arms and legs. All around me, sleepy voices muttered. The sun came up. It shimmered like a ball of fire on the spires of the cathedral.

Two mornings ago, I saw the same sun rise above a daisy meadow in Missouri. Here in Jackson Square there were no daisies, only dented cans and jagged shards of glass. Yet it was the same sun, announcing a new day in the same spectacular style.

"Hey, Wisconsin! I was right!" Zil called. "I knew you'd bring me luck."

She bounded toward me, leaping over Tomato's outstretched legs. She waved a torn, flapping billfold. "It was laying right on the sidewalk!" she exclaimed. "There's twelve dollars in it!"

She flopped down beside me and counted out the bills — a wrinkled five and seven ones. It was as if she had found buried treasure.

"Hey, know what else?" she asked. "I found your Sister What's-her-name."

"You did!" I cried. "Sister Euphrasia?"

"Yeah, that's the one. While you were sleeping. I went around asking everybody. Fangs knows her."

"Where is she?" I was on my feet, ready to get started.

"It's not too far." Zil hesitated. "Only she said — this sister's not like — she's not what you'd think."

"What do you mean?" I asked. A cold lump of dread lodged in my chest. After all my searching, Sister Euphrasia was a fake. She wouldn't be able to help me. I would go back to Madison with nothing to show for everyone's trouble.

"She might not want to see you," Zil said. "She's famous or something."

"I know," I said. "That's how I heard of her."

"Yeah, but it's like — she was on TV one time," Zil argued. "She must charge a lot of money." She paused. With an effort she added, "You can have my twelve dollars, if it'll help."

Tears sprang to my eyes. Godzilla ate out of

garbage cans. But she was ready to hand me all her newfound wealth. "No, you don't need to do that," I assured her. "I'll work it out somehow."

But how? I wondered. Had I come so far, just to be turned aside because I couldn't pay? If only I'd won first prize instead of second in the drawing contest! If only I hadn't been robbed on the train! If only . . .

I ran my fingers over the lump in my neck. It was bigger, without a doubt.

"If you want to go, I'll take you," Zil promised.

16

With some of my dwindling funds, I bought us both breakfast at a tiny café. We had hot, deep-fried doughnuts covered with powdered sugar. Zil called them *bengnets*, and said they were a special New Orleans treat. The sugar spattered our faces and clothes, and we had to brush ourselves off when we got back out to the sidewalk. "You bring me luck and more luck," Zil told me. "I haven't had bengnets all week!"

On the way to Sister Euphrasia's place, Zil took a shortcut through alleys, over fences, and across backyards. Once a big German shepherd hurled himself to the end of his chain, trying to chew us up. Laughing, Zil danced within inches of his snapping jaws.

"Vwah-lah!" she said with satisfaction. "Here it is!"

We stood before a high gate, its wrought-iron patterns painted a faded green. Through the leaves and curlicues I saw a long hallway filled with hanging plants. The name by the bell was Castalet.

"Are you sure this is it?" I asked. "It doesn't look right."

"Chartres Street, the green gate on the corner," Zil said. "Fangs knows."

"I thought it would be different." I'd pictured a shabby storefront, or maybe a sparkling office like the ones at the clinic in Madison. I had never imagined this elaborate green gate, this profusion of flowering plants. And the name was wrong. Why wasn't Sister Euphrasia's name posted on a sign for the world to see?

But this had to be the place. Chartres Street . . . green gate . . .

My heart raced. I couldn't breathe. I couldn't lift my hand to press the bell.

"You getting bad vibes?" Zil asked. "Want to cut out?"

I shook my head and forced myself to breathe steadily. I raised my hand. Somewhere at the far end of the passage, a bell chimed.

I turned to Zil. "You're coming in with me, right?" I asked.

She drew back, aghast. "No way!" she said. "Not me!"

"I can't go alone!" I protested.

Zil retreated a few steps up the street. She spread her hand, trying for a moment to hide the tattoos on her arm. When she spoke, her voice was low and shaken. "I can't go in a fancy rich house like that," she said. "I can't."

Somewhere out of sight, a door rattled open. A dog yapped, and footsteps hurried toward us. "Please!" I begged.

"Sorry," Zil said. "I'm out of here." There *were* things that frightened her after all. Nothing I could say would make a difference.

"See you back at the square," she called over her shoulder. "I've got to look for more states!"

Another door opened, closer this time. The dog scampered into view, a schnauzer. It nearly lost its balance, skidding toward me across the tiled entryway. Barking joyfully, tail wagging, it leaped against the gate.

"Casey, cut it out!" a woman's voice called. A figure stepped into the passage, hurrying forward to seize the dog by the collar. It was a woman, dressed in jeans and a paint-spattered smock. She was short and compact, with a solid, down-to-earth expression. She could easily be somebody's mother. She looked at me questioningly.

"I think I'm at the wrong house," I said. "I was looking for this lady called — " The name sounded so preposterous I didn't want to say it aloud. "Never mind," I said. I began to turn away.

The woman scooped Casey up and held him in her arms. "Who are you looking for?" she asked.

"Someone I heard about," I said. She kept studying me until I added, "They called her Sister Euphrasia."

The woman smiled and unfastened the gate. "Well," she said, "you've come to the right place."

"Does she really live here?" I said, stepping inside.

"Yes, she does," the woman said. "You want Sister Euphrasia? That's me."

My mother always told me it's rude to stare, but I couldn't help it. She looked so ordinary, like one of our neighbors down the street. Her shoulder-length hair was a soft honey-brown, and she pulled it back with a red bandanna. She wore no jewelry, and no makeup. "I thought you might be the plumber," she said, fastening the gate behind me. "I've got a bit of an emergency. There's a major leak in the bathroom. This guy said he'd come, even though it's Sunday."

I couldn't quite believe that this was the person I had traveled such a distance to see. I couldn't believe that she was the famous Sister Euphrasia.

"Come on," she said. "Let's go out to the kitchen where we can talk."

I followed her down the covered passage and into a wide, sunny courtyard. A canary sang merrily from a hanging cage. Across the courtyard lay the living area of the house. "Okay," she said, when we were settled at the kitchen table. "Tell me why you're here."

"If you're really Sister Euphrasia, how come the name out there is Castalet?" I asked.

"Euphrasia Castalet, that's my name," she said. "I go by Sister. In the work I do, it feels right somehow."

"Do you really cure people?" I asked. "Like, if somebody's got a bad disease?"

Sister Euphrasia gazed down at her hands. She thought for a long moment before she answered. "Sometimes I'm given the chance to help."

"Can you help me?" I said in a rush. "I've got Hodgkin's disease. And I don't want to go back in the hospital for more treatment. That's worse than dying!"

"You have Hodgkin's disease," she repeated. "You've been in treatment?"

"For three years," I said. "I thought I was in remission now, but" — I struggled to bring out the words — "but now I think I've got another tumor." Gingerly I touched the place on my neck again.

"What do you know about me?" Sister Euphrasia asked. "What do you think is going to happen?"

"Kim told me," I explained. "She's this girl I met at my doctor's office. She said you just touch people and they get better. All these scientists came and proved it. Kim said you have a gift."

"That's what it is," she said, nodding. "The thing about a gift is, you can't demand it. And you don't control it. You can ask, and hope, and sometimes it's given."

I didn't understand what she meant. I felt shaky all over, as if my chills were coming back. "Have you got the gift today? Can you cure *me*?"

"I don't know," she said. "I never do, until I try."

"I've got money," I told her desperately. "I have my return ticket, so I can give you everything that's left."

"I don't take payment," she said, laughing a little. "You can't charge for a gift, can you?"

"No," I said, "I guess you can't."

Sister Euphrasia said she would need some time to herself, "to meditate." "You can wait in the treatment room," she said. "Try to think quiet thoughts. Think about things that make you happy."

The treatment room, as she called it, opened off the courtyard. It was small and bright, with woven rugs on the floor and a scattering of beanbag chairs. In the center stood a low table covered with blankets. There were no file cabinets, no cold medical instruments, no rolls of sterile gauze. No diplomas hung on the walls, only a large watercolor of waves on a beach.

I chose one of the beanbag chairs, and rustled into a comfortable position. Outside, the canary trilled and whistled. I looked at the seascape on the wall and tried to think of things that made me happy. But my mind wouldn't stay still. Was this my journey's end, this little room full of sunlight? This woman who waited for the plumber? How could she possibly drive out the illness that had its grip on me?

Think quiet thoughts, I told myself sternly. I might ruin everything if I didn't follow Sister Euphrasia's directions.

Ruin what? I taunted myself. She had no magic. She was a snake-oil seller after all.

But she wasn't selling anything. She said you couldn't charge for a gift.

I tried to think of something peaceful and pleasant. The seascape didn't help. It reminded me of Aunt Kath's place on Lake Michigan. I should have gone with Mom Thursday morning. I should have spent the day splashing and sunning, and forgotten my crazy idea of running away to New Orleans. Soon, very soon now, I would have to head home. I'd have to answer all of my parents' questions and reproaches. I had done an unforgivable thing, and I could never show them how sorry I was.

I closed my eyes and looked for another picture to fill my mind. I thought of my eleventh birthday, the last one before I got sick. I remembered my best present, real drawing classes at a young people's art program. I had been so excited, so sure I would become a great artist someday. I never guessed that disaster would befall me, that my whole life would be overturned by one visit to the doctor.

Couldn't I remember anything without sadness and worry? Wasn't there any picture that brought me happy feelings?

Suddenly I thought of Zil, offering me the money she had found on the sidewalk. I remembered Miss Rebecca Tilden, rushing forward to rescue me from Norma Jean. I thought of Blake, waving from the platform as my train pulled out of the station. Those memories gave me a warm glow. I had set out on this journey alone. But all along the way I had found wonderful friends.

"Are you ready now?" Sister Euphrasia stood in the doorway. She had changed into a long, loose dress with a soft flower print. She shut the door behind her and drew the curtains, darkening the room. The canary's song still reached me, delicate and far away.

"Take your shoes off and lie down on the table," Sister Euphrasia said.

I kicked off my sandals and stretched out. "What if the plumber shows up?" I asked. "Will you stop and let him in?"

For a moment she seemed bewildered, as though she didn't know what I was talking about. "Oh," she said at last. "It's all right. I disconnected the bell."

She walked toward me slowly, with surprising

grace. She was like a dancer, I thought, performing a ballet with long, flowing gestures. She stopped beside the table and spread her hands above my body. "Close your eyes," she said. "Fill your mind with peace."

I lay without moving. Eyes closed, I listened to the stillness around me. I heard the swish of Sister Euphrasia's dress as she moved. I felt the tiny shift in the air as she bent above me. She had become someone new and extraordinary, a presence I had never experienced before. She seemed to hover somewhere in the air, as if the law of gravity meant nothing any longer and she had broken free of the floor.

A deep calm washed through me. My worries didn't vanish, but they withdrew. I felt certain that somehow everything would be all right.

Lightly, gently, Sister Euphrasia's fingers brushed over my throat. They paused for a long time at the place where the lump had appeared. Afterwards, their warmth lingered on.

I don't know how long I lay there, half awake, half dreaming. At last Sister Euphrasia touched my shoulder. "You can sit up now," she said. "We're finished."

She opened the curtains, and the sun flooded in once more. "What happened?" I asked, dazed. "Am I better?"

"What you have is in hiding," she said. "It is beyond my reach."

She opened the door. The canary poured forth a fresh burst of song.

"What do you mean?" I asked cautiously. "It's in hiding?"

"Yes," she said. Her voice was tinged with sorrow. "I wish I could do something for you. But I don't have the power to take your cancer away."

I sank onto the table and covered my face with my hands. I had made the long trip for nothing. My cancer was incurable after all. I was a hopeless case, doomed to die. No one could help me, nobody on earth.

I didn't bother to fight the tears. Nothing mattered anymore. There was nowhere left for me to go. I swayed back and forth, sobbing out my despair.

I was dimly aware of Sister Euphrasia beside me. She put her hand on my shoulder. Her touch was ordinary now, without that mysterious, healing warmth. But gradually, my tears stopped and I turned to meet her gaze. "I can't cure you," she said. "But I think the doctors can."

"I've already been through three years of treatment," I said.

"You need to go back," she told me. "You won't be able to leap past the treatment. You have to go through it all. The only way out is through."

From the courtyard, Casey broke into a frenzy of yapping. "That might be the plumber," Sister Euphrasia said. "Casey's letting me know."

I trailed behind her across the courtyard and down the hallway. She belonged to the real world again, the world of leaking pipes. She grabbed Casey, opened the gate, and let the plumber in.

"Good-bye," I said. "And thank you."

"Don't give up," she said. "There's still a way out for you."

She gave me a hug with one arm — the other one held Casey. "Good-bye," I said again. Once more I was on the street, alone.

17

The sun blazed down without any mercy. I trudged along until I grew tired. Then I rested until I could no longer sit still, and had to start walking again. I bought a hot dog from a stand on a street corner, but I could barely taste it. It didn't matter what I ate or where I wandered.

When I finally thought to check my watch, it was past noon. I dug out my ticket and discovered that my train left at seven P.M. I'd get to Chicago tomorrow afternoon, and catch a bus back to Madison. It would all take a long time. But time didn't matter, either.

With an effort I dragged my thoughts backward, past my visit to Sister Euphrasia. Zil had said she'd meet me in Jackson Square. I had to find her. I needed to thank her for her help, and tell her good-bye.

I didn't know my way around the French Quarter, but Jackson Square was too big to miss. The saxophone player was back; I recognized him from the night before. I saw a couple of the kids I camped out with, too. I didn't know their names, and they didn't seem to remember me. We passed each other without speaking. I bought some pretzels from a street vendor, and sat on a bench to wait. Sooner or later Zil would come. Her home was Jackson Square.

I got up and circled the park, but I didn't see Zil anywhere. The saxophone player launched into a jazzy tune, but nobody paid him much attention. I felt a little sorry for him, and sat on the grass to listen.

"Hey! Hey, Sis, there you are!"

I ignored the voice, and clapped as the saxophone player finished with a flourish.

"It's me, Sis! Don't you remember?" A tall, slim boy with a blue backpack strode toward me. He waved a bandaged hand. But it couldn't be. . . . Blake was in Denver by now. . . .

"Shannon Thomas! It's me! Blake!"

There he stood, grinning as if I really was his long-lost sister. He held out his arms. I sprang to my feet and dashed to meet him. Blake swept me into a joyful hug and danced me over the grass. My feet hardly seemed to touch the ground.

"What are you doing here?" I cried. "You're supposed to be in Colorado!"

"I'm here instead," he said, laughing. "I caught the Greyhound and got in last night."

I couldn't quite take it in. I kept staring at him, as if he might vanish. "Why?" I asked. "What made you come here?"

Blake took both my hands and stepped back to look at me. "I came here," he said, "to hunt for you."

We found a bench by Andrew Jackson, and Blake told me his story. It was simple, really. After he saw me off back in Chicago, he spent Thursday night at the train station. He planned to take the three-o'clock train to Denver on Friday afternoon. But in the morning he bought a newspaper, and there was the headline about the girl with cancer who had run away. He recognized me, even with the wig.

"I didn't have to go to Denver," he explained. "It was just the only place I could think of. The second I figured out who you were, I knew what I had to do."

My excitement dimmed. If Blake read the newspaper story, he knew about the reward. Maybe he had rushed to New Orleans to claim his five thousand dollars. It would help him pay his father back for the car.

"Did you call anybody?" I asked. "Did you tell them you knew where I was?"

He looked blank. "Tell who?"

"The police. My parents. Anybody."

Blake shook his head, frowning. "What for? It was *you* I had to find."

"Well, here I am." I waited, half expecting him to dash for the nearest phone booth. But he didn't move. He sat on the bench, looking at me intently.

"Why did you come down here?" he asked. "Your folks are really worried, you know."

"I left them a message," I said, trying to defend myself.

"Yeah, but how do they know you're not kidnapped or something? Maybe somebody made you say that stuff. Maybe they had a gun to your head."

"I never thought of that."

"I bet your folks did!"

Somehow I had to explain myself. I told him about Dr. Calder, and how he said my remission was borderline and wanted me to have more chemotherapy. I told him about Kim, and her promise that there was a way out. I described leaving home, and my adventures along the way. And finally I told him about Sister Euphrasia. "So after all that, the whole trip was for nothing," I said. My voice was shaky with tears.

"What do you mean? You figured out what to do, didn't you?"

I guess it was my turn to look blank. I couldn't imagine what he meant.

"She told you that you still have cancer, but she gave you the way out," Blake said. "You better get home and get started."

"I'm going," I told him. "I've got my return ticket."

"You're going to let them go on worrying and searching till you show up tomorrow night?" Blake demanded. "Don't you think you ought to tell them you're on your way?"

"Hey!" I exclaimed. "You're a great one to talk! You're not in any hurry to call *your* folks. I bet they're just as frantic as mine."

"Yeah. Right." A note of bitterness crept into Blake's voice. "I don't see anything in the papers about a nationwide search for me!"

"You're not sick," I said. "You don't make good press. The reporters would probably say there are a thousand runaway kids every week."

"You don't know my dad," Blake said. "He doesn't want me back. He'll never forgive me for wrecking his Mercedes."

The thought of calling home filled me with dread. I didn't know what I could say to make up for the pain I had caused. Yet I knew that my family missed me and wanted me. I was certain that they would welcome me back.

It must be so much harder for Blake. If he called home, he didn't know what kind of reception he would get. He was so afraid, he'd rather wander the country forever.

"Listen," I said, "let's make a deal. I'll call my folks, and you call yours — and then let's get something to eat!"

"It's not that easy," Blake said. "My dad's got a real fierce temper."

"The worst he can do is scream at you," I pointed out. "You ought to try at least. See what happens."

Blake was quiet for a while. I wished I could read his thoughts. At last he said, "You call yours first," and I knew he had made a decision.

Together Blake and I set off in search of a pay phone. As we crossed the square, Zil sauntered toward us. "Hey, Wisconsin! How'd it go?"

"She was really okay," I said. "Even if she *is* famous."

Out of the corner of my eye, I noticed Blake staring. He was seeing her for the first time, the way I saw her last night.

I introduced them with a little curtsey, as if we were at a formal tea. "Blake, this is my friend Godzilla. Zil, this is Blake."

They eyed each other for a moment, taking each other's measure. Finally Blake reached out his hand.

"Hey, Blake," Zil said. "Where are you from?"

"Illinois," he told her.

Her face fell. "Illinois!" she groaned. "You're the third one this week!"

I knew we had to keep moving, before our courage failed. "We've got to go," I told her. "I don't know if I'll see you anymore. I guess I better say good-bye."

"People come and people go," she said flatly. "See you."

"Listen," I said, before she could turn away. "Thanks for everything. You helped me an awful lot."

"I did?" she exclaimed, and her grin was back, bigger than ever.

After we said our good-byes, Blake and I found a little seafood restaurant that had a couple of pay phones. He watched as I counted out my change. "Forget that!" he said, laughing. "Call collect. I think they'll accept the charges."

I stepped into the booth and slid the door shut. It was hot and stuffy inside. But I didn't want anyone to overhear me, not even Blake. I punched "O" and placed a collect call to our house in Madison.

Mom picked up the phone on the second ring. "Thomas residence," she said, her voice clipped and businesslike. She must have been taking calls for three days — from detectives, from neighbors, from curious strangers.

"Mom?" I began, but an automated voice broke in, asking her if she would take the call. "Yes yes *yes*!" she shouted. "Shannon? Shannon! Is it you?"

"Yeah, it's me," I said. And for a few moments neither of us said anything more. I think we were both crying.

"It's Shannon!" Mom yelled to someone, and a moment later Dad picked up the extension.

"Where are you?" he asked, as soon as he was sure it was really me.

"I'm in New Orleans," I said. "I'm coming home on the train."

"Then it's true!" Mom said. "That boy told us you must have gone to New Orleans. He was right!"

"What boy?" I asked. "Nobody could have known but Kim."

"This was a boy," Mom said. "Jonathan Smith. He called up and — "

"Oh!" I exclaimed. "Kim's brother! I remember now!"

"Where exactly are you this minute?" Dad broke in. "What's the phone number there?"

I read him the number of the pay phone, and he repeated it twice to be sure he had it right. They both said no, absolutely not, I wasn't taking the train home by myself. It was too far. It was just too dangerous.

"Hey! I got all the way down here alone," I protested. But somehow they didn't see the humor.

"Shannon, why did you do this?" Mom asked again. "Don't you know how worried we've been?"

"I had to come," I said. "I was trying to get cured."

I sketched in the story of Sister Euphrasia, without going into detail. They listened in silence.

"Stay on the phone," Dad said. "I'm going to

make a call from the line in Mom's office."

"Who's he talking to?" I asked Mom, when it was just the two of us again.

She said she wasn't sure, and asked me a lot of questions about what I'd been eating and whether I got any sleep. I didn't tell her about my night in Jackson Square. I had a feeling I never would.

"Mom," I said at last, taking a deep breath, "are they still expecting me at the hospital Thursday?"

"Thursday?" she said. "I don't know. I haven't thought that far ahead in so long. . . . I've been living hour to hour for the past three days."

"Well, if they are — I guess I've got to go in. I just have to go through it."

From the booth next door, coins rattled into the box. Blake's voice murmured indistinctly. I strained to catch his words, but they were muffled by the walls between us.

"We'll work that out," Mom was saying in my ear. "Just get home safely!"

Dad picked up the extension again. "You're coming in on the next plane," he announced. "The New Orleans police will escort you to the airport."

Even as he spoke, two uniformed officers pushed through the restaurant door. One of them rapped on the glass of my booth. "I guess I better go," I said. "They're here."

18

One of the officers showed me his badge. His name was Sergeant McCarthy. "Miss Thomas?" he inquired.

The other policeman, Sergeant Duchenne, was a little older. He looked as if he was having a good time. Probably he spent most days arresting jewel thieves and hired assassins. Nabbing me must have been like taking a field trip. He grinned at me and held out his hand. "You *are* Shannon Thomas, aren't you?" he asked.

For an instant I wanted to say no. I had been so many people over the past three days: Louisa Pritchard, Wisconsin, and just plain Sis. I had grown used to inventing new identities. But I had to be me again.

My old shyness crept back along with my name. I felt myself blush. "I'm Shannon," I admitted.

I shook Sergeant Duchenne's hand, and his grin grew even broader. "We're taking you to catch a plane," he said. "I bet you never rode in a squad car before."

"Wait!" I protested. I pointed toward the phone booth where Blake still stood, framed behind the glass door. I couldn't see his face, but he was deep in conversation.

Sergeant McCarthy frowned. "We've got to put you on a six-ten flight. It's the last one out tonight."

"I can't go yet!" I said. "My friend is in there. I can't walk off and leave him!"

Was this what they called "resisting arrest"? I'd never ridden in a squad car, but I knew one thing about the police. When they told you to do something, you weren't supposed to argue. Still, Blake had come all the way to New Orleans to find me. He hadn't tried to cash in on the reward. He just wanted to make sure I got home safely. I had to do the same for him. Maybe I wasn't such a mouse after all.

"The kid in there?" Sergeant Duchenne asked. "Is he with you?"

At that point, the glass door slid open, and Blake emerged. His face was beaded with sweat. He looked from me to the officers, and back at me again. "Hey," he said at last. "What's going on?"

So much had happened since I placed my collect call. I wanted Blake to know everything I had said and everything my parents had said to me. But when I opened my mouth, I simply told him, "I'm going home."

Blake nodded his understanding. "Me, too," he said.

Sergeant Duchenne turned to his partner. "Shannon's got plenty of time to get to the airport," he declared. "These kids need food before they go anywhere!"

That's how I finally ate in a New Orleans restaurant. Sergeant Duchenne and Sergeant McCarthy said we couldn't leave town without sampling some genuine boiled crawfish, and ordered a platter of them for all of us to share. The crawfish came whole, right down to their claws and eyes and antennae. I can't say they were an appetizing sight at first. Sergeant Duchenne showed us how to snap off the tails, peel away the shell, and devour the morsel of meat inside. It was a messy business, but pretty soon I didn't care. I was hungry enough to eat anything that would hold still.

In a few more days I'd be in the hospital again. They'd pump more chemicals into my veins, and I would feel too sick to lift my head. The thought of food would be repulsive. I'd better eat now, while I had the chance.

As time passed, Blake began to relax. Over a growing mound of empty shells, he told us about his call home. His father had done plenty of hollering. But just as Blake was ready to hang up the phone, he suddenly fell silent. "I thought maybe we were disconnected," Blake marveled. "And then he said to me, 'Oh, what's a car, anyway? Just a pile of sheet metal! I want you to come home!' " I wasn't sure, but I thought I saw tears in Blake's eyes.

"Are you taking the train again?" I asked. *"The City of New Orleans*? You can have my return ticket."

"That's such a long trip," Sergeant Duchenne said. "Maybe we can cash in that ticket and put you on a plane, too."

"We're not exactly in the travel business, but I guess we can help make arrangements," Sergeant McCarthy put in gruffly. By now, even he was starting to smile, as if he were enjoying a holiday.

After our meal, there were a lot of phone calls. I called home to tell Mom and Dad that the police had found me and were taking me to the airport. Then Sergeant McCarthy talked to Blake's dad. I don't know how they worked it out, but after a few more calls, Blake had a plane reservation to Springfield, by way of St. Louis. My own flight had a layover in Chicago. Neither one of us would be home until midnight.

We rode to the airport in the back of the squad car. Sergeant Duchenne threatened to clamp us into handcuffs, just for fun, and we all laughed. Sergeant McCarthy pointed out the Mississippi River, wide and brown beyond the window. "You can't visit New Orleans without saying hello to the Big Muddy," he said.

Once we got to the airport, though, our spirits faded. It was time to say good-bye. "Is Blake your first name or your last name?" I asked as we stood in the check-in line. "You never did tell me."

"Neither," he said. "Michael Blake Coleman."

"You mean they call you Michael at home?"

"No," he said. "Actually, at home I'm Junior."

"I'll always think of you as Blake," I said. I wondered if I would ever see him again.

My flight was the first to depart. They all escorted me to my gate and waited with me until boarding time. Blake and I had a lot to think about. For a little while, waiting for the boarding announcement, neither one of us felt alone.

It took me almost three days to get from Madison to New Orleans. Even with the change of planes in Chicago my trip back to Madison was dizzyingly fast. As we slid into the descent, my hands went clammy with panic. I wasn't ready to face Mom and Dad yet. I needed a few more hours to figure out what to say to them. But the FASTEN SEATBELTS sign flashed on, and with a jolting bump we were on the ground.

I picked up my purse and backpack. I'd been carrying them for so long that they felt like part of my body. My heart raced, but my feet moved reluctantly down the narrow aisle. I saw my parents as I climbed down the steps. Mom and Dad hurried toward me, arms outstretched. Behind them, Cousin Rena toted an enormous WELCOME HOME sign. Aunt Kath was there with a big bouquet. A strange woman, whom I recognized right away as a reporter, pointed her camera this way and that. She was capturing the whole scene on film.

"Shannon!" Mom cried, catching me in a long, fierce hug. "You're here! Thank God!"

It was Dad's turn next. He was so choked up he could hardly speak at all.

The only person who demanded answers that night was Maggie Sinclair, the reporter from Channel 14 News. As I hurried down the concourse she stuck a microphone in front of my face and asked, "Did you know you were a national celebrity?"

"I knew I was in the papers, yeah."

"That was quite a trip you took all by yourself. Can you tell us anything about it?"

"I made some really good friends," I said. I thought of Sister Euphrasia, and struggled for the right words. "I didn't get cured, though. I guess for me there isn't an easy way out."

I guess she didn't know what to say to that, so she moved on down her list of questions. "How does it feel to be back?"

Everyone beamed at me — Mom and Dad, Cousin Rena and Aunt Kath. I grinned back at them. "It's great to be back," I said. "I'm really glad to be home again!"

The next day, Monday, I slept until almost noon. When I finally staggered down to the kitchen, Mom emerged from her office to greet me. It was the first time we'd been alone together since I got back. I knew I was in for a heavy discussion. Since I couldn't avoid it, I was determined to get it out of the way.

For a few minutes, we focused on food. I cooked French toast, a lifetime favorite. Mom made us a big fruit salad, with peaches and grapes, orange sections and chunks of watermelon. It worked as the opener I needed. "While I was gone, the only healthy breakfast I got was with the Bennetts," I said.

"Who are the Bennetts?" Mom wanted to know. So I told her about traveling with the gospel choir, and the generous people who fed us and let us take showers. Chapter by chapter, the trip unfolded, until at last I reached the French Quarter.

It wasn't the kind of story most mothers relish. My mom was no exception. She kept moaning, "Oh, no!" and "Don't tell me!" But I knew she really wanted to hear it all. I had to tell her.

I knew she couldn't handle the story of the picnic behind Pierre's Restaurant, though. I hoped she wouldn't ask where I slept that night in New Orleans. "I saw in the paper about the reward," I said. "I kept worrying about you and Dad, what you were going through."

"We were sure glad you left that message on your dad's answering machine," Mom said. "After that I had the feeling everything was going to be all right."

"Mom," I asked, "who put up all that reward money? Five thousand dollars! That's a lot!"

"Everybody pitched in," Mom said. "Aunt Kath and Cousin Rena, Abby's parents, some people from church, some teachers from your art program. People kept calling and asking how they could help."

I thought about that for a while, as I served myself some more fruit salad. It was hard to absorb the fact that so many people really cared. "What will happen to the money now?" I asked at last.

"I suppose it should go to Jonathan Smith," Mom said. "Because of him, we contacted the TV stations in the New Orleans area. They gave us a lot of coverage."

"That must be why those nurses guessed who I was," I said. "I wouldn't tell them anything, but they knew."

"There was a woman who called from Chicago," Mom added. "She said she met you on the bus from Madison. You drew a picture of her little boy."

I remembered her, with her smiling black-haired baby. That had been Thursday morning. It seemed so very long ago. "Really," I said, "Blake was the one who found me. He went all the way to New Orleans to look for me."

"We'll think about that," Mom said.

"You know," I told her, "Sister Euphrasia was really nice, but she didn't have the answer," I said sadly. "I'm back where I started."

Mom sighed. "I made you an appointment with Dr. Calder. This afternoon at four o'clock."

"Shannon Thomas!" the receptionist greeted me. She finally had my name right. I guess she couldn't help it, after hearing it on TV every night.

Everyone in the waiting room stared. "I'm so glad they found you, dear!" said an old woman with white hair. "I heard all about you on the news this morning." I used to think it would be fun to be famous. Now I know it's embarrassing more than anything else.

At first, Dr. Calder acted embarrassed, too. After all, I was the patient who made headlines by running away from his treatment plan. Considering the bad press I gave him, he was surprisingly good-natured. "Well," he said, "I understand you're not terribly fond of the hospital."

"Not terribly, no!" I said.

"I've been talking to an old friend of yours," he

179

went on. "Dr. O'Brien out in California. I'm faxing her your latest lab work. We want to think about it together. We need to make the right decision."

"I know what the decision is," I said wearily. "There's a funny lump on my neck you need to look at."

Abby called that night. She wanted to know all about my adventures, and we talked for a long time. Almost as soon as I hung up, I got a call from Kim Smith. "You beat me to it!" she cried. "My mom's still scraping up money for our tickets!"

"Sister Euphrasia's a really neat lady," I said. "I can't describe how she made me feel. Peaceful. I guess that was it. For a little while, when I was there, I felt perfectly peaceful."

"My brother thinks we're crazy, but we're going," Kim said. "I've got to find out."

I wished her luck. "When you see her," I said, "give her my love."

Over the next few days, there were a lot of calls to labs and doctors. Regretfully, everyone agreed that the numbers weren't what they ought to be, according to the new Houston study. Besides, that new lump on my neck was proof that I needed treatment. I wasn't in a good, strong remission after all. There was more work to be done.

Only a week ago I had felt outraged and discouraged at the thought of returning to the hospital. It didn't seem I could survive. Now somehow the prospect no longer overwhelmed me. Chemotherapy would be unpleasant, but in the end I would put it behind me. When Dr. Calder told me I simply *had* to undergo more treatment, I listened calmly.

19

It was late March when I read the announcement in the paper. They were coming to Madison, the Angel Voices Gospel Choir! "This would be a nice occasion to invite the Colemans up from Illinois," Mom suggested.

I jumped at the idea. I got Blake on the phone that very night. He sounded great, and I knew he was glad to hear from me. He was saving the reward money so he could go to trade school; he wanted to study cooking. "One of these days I'll become a great New Orleans chef!" he promised. "You can eat in my restaurant for free."

"And we'll invite Godzilla," I said. "I'd sure love to find her someday."

They all came up for the weekend — Blake and his parents and his two little sisters. The house was full of happy confusion, like when all my aunts and cousins come for Thanksgiving dinner. Mom and Dad had never met Blake before, and I was a little worried about how everyone would get along. But it felt as though we'd all known each other forever. We had just acquired a new set of relatives.

The concert was held in a church a few blocks from our house. Sitting in a back pew, I let the songs pour over me: "Amazing Grace," "Shall We Gather by the River?," and all the others. I remembered that morning in the meadow, and my eyes filled with tears.

Afterward I took Mom and Dad up to the front to meet Miss Rebecca Tilden. "Well!" she exclaimed. "If it isn't Louisa Grace Pritchard!"

"Actually, they call me Shannon Thomas," I told her.

"Whatever they call you," Miss Tilden said, "I knew you were a fine young lady the moment I saw you."

Mom gave her a big hug. "Shannon's told us so much about you," she said. "We're so grateful to you for taking care of her."

"My pleasure," Miss Tilden said. "Get her to sing a scale now and then. It's good for the soul."

As everyone piled into the car, Blake and I volunteered to walk back to the house. It gave us a good chance to talk alone. "Your dad is really nice," I told him, a little surprised. "It seems like you get along pretty well now."

"He's mellowed," Blake said. He paused and added, "I guess I have, too."

"I think I lived ten years in those three days

last summer," I said. "I still think about it all the time. There's so much to remember, and try to understand."

"Was your treatment awful?" Blake asked hesitantly.

I kicked at a stone on the sidewalk. "It was pretty ugly, yeah. But now they're getting really good numbers from my blood and my bone marrow and all those tests."

"Does that mean you're cured?"

I shook my head. "They never say that word. It's a jinx."

"So you're right where you were before, then," Blake said. He didn't quite look at me.

"No," I said, "it's different now. I felt uncertain before, as if I had no future. And now — " I searched for a way to explain. "Now I really believe I'll have time."

"You look healthy," Blake said. "Do you feel better?"

"A lot! I don't feel like a mouse anymore!"

"You?" Blake exclaimed. "A kid who could go off to New Orleans alone, and find somebody when you didn't know their address or even their full name — you were never a mouse!"

"I used to be," I said. "That trip changed me. I'm not afraid of people anymore."

"You never acted shy when I met you," Blake said. "I remember you chasing me down the street."

"A weird thing happened the other night," I told him. "I baby-sat for this spoiled little girl. She started making a fuss at bedtime and I said, 'Virginia, that's enough!' And that's all it took. It was never that way before."

Blake wasn't impressed. He thrust his hands into his pockets, and pulled out a pair of gloves. "It's cold up here in Wisconsin!" he grumbled. "How do you stand it, Sis?"

"Not very well," I said. "Come on." I grabbed his hand, and together we ran the last block home.